ELKE FEUER

DEADLY
BLOODLINES

For more information on the author and her works, please see http://elkefeuer.com

To my wonderful husband, who has turned out to be the Prince Charming I always knew he was, and to my Creator, who continues to bless me beyond belief, even when I don't deserve it.

TABLE OF CONTENTS

ACKNOWLEDGMENTS

This book would not have gotten into the hands of readers without the help of all these people, starting with Katie Crowley, my best friend and best critique partner ever, and beta readers Alan and John.

To Francine LaSala (francinelasalaproductions. wordpress.com) for her wonderful copyediting and Faith Williams (http://www.theatwatergroup.com/Meet%20Faith. html) from The Atwater Group, who did an awesome job of proofreading my novel, thanks for making my book shine like a diamond in the sun.

Special thanks to Kari at Cover to Cover Designs (http://www.covertocoverdesigns.com) for my totally awesome book cover.

Thanks to Dr. Joy Ti and his forensic staff at the George Town Hospital for answering my countless questions, and for allowing me to observe while they worked, and to Derek Haines for giving me a peek behind Cayman's police procedures and answering my endless questions.

i

PROLOGUE

There she is!

Sweat covered his palms as she stepped out her front door. His heart beat wildly and his breath hitched in his chest, as if someone had punched him in the stomach. Only she had that power over him. A power she had held the moment he first saw her.

She locked her apartment door and headed down the stairs to the ground floor of the building. Her hair was pulled into a ponytail, making him wonder why she never let it down. She had shoulder-length, beautiful ebony hair he knew would feel soft beneath his fingertips, and smell like the sea she loved to swim in at night. Many nights he watched her swim, her lean body moving through the dark water that was sometimes kissed by the reflection of moonlight. Those were the nights he looked forward to, that he longed for. That slight smile she wore on her face when she finished swimming.

He didn't judge her past. It was what he liked most about her; what drew him to her.

She got into her car and drove away without seeing him. It didn't matter; he planned it that way. He started his car and let his fingertips stroke the smooth leather of the steering wheel from one side to the other, imagining it was her skin, before gripping it tightly.

Soon. Soon she'd be his.

1

CHAPTER 1

Angel Mason sat on the edge of her bed and squished the thick caramel carpet between her toes, assurance the deadly grip of another nightmare was gone.

On the nightstand her phone vibrated, startling her. It was Dustin Williams, Chief Superintendent. The time, 6:30 a.m., flashed in red from her clock. She cleared her throat and prayed there was no trace of the bottle of vodka she'd finished off the night before in her voice. "Inspector Angel."

"Dead body at Galleon Bay." He never minced words.

"Some tourist die in their sleep?"

"No, looks like she was murdered."

Brittle silence hung in the air as the words echoed in her mind like a broken record.

"Angel?"

"I'll be there in half an hour," she stammered.

"Good, I want this dealt with quickly. There hasn't been a tourist murdered on the island since…"

"Since Meredith," she finished for him.

"Yeah, and we remember how that turned out," he said dryly.

The phone imprinted her hand as she squeezed it. No one had forgotten how it turned out, least of all her—no matter how hard she tried.

"I want you to collect the evidence," Williams said.

"What? Why?" She didn't normally question his

3

decisions, but she hadn't worked in forensics since she had been promoted to inspector.

"You're the most experienced scene of crime officer we have."

"I'll take care of it, sir," Angel assured him.

"Johnson, Sanchez, and Ebanks are already there controlling the traffic and crowd," he said, his voice sounding miles away.

"Yes, sir."

The phone went dead without a goodbye, not that she expected one. He didn't converse beyond necessity, but she never took it personally. He was like that with everyone.

She went to the bathroom, took out the bottle of painkillers on the second shelf of the cabinet on the wall, and downed two.

As the pills made their way to her queasy stomach, she searched the cloud in her head for how she had gotten to bed last night. Leftover Chinese and drifting to sleep during the nightly news in a vodka-induced haze was all she remembered.

Horrifying screams and blood splattered across her hand paraded before her, remaining trickles from her dream, and the smell of blood filled her nose.

"No!" She gripped the edges of the porcelain sink to steady herself and clear her mind of the images. Her dreams were becoming more frequent and the vivid details lingering long after she awoke.

She let out the breath she was holding and splashed cold water on her face. The reflection in the mirror was an unwanted reminder that she couldn't escape her heritage or the history that came with it, and there was nothing she could do about it.

Once she showered and got dressed, she pulled her hair into a ponytail. She walked down the short beige corridor to the living room and grabbed her keys off the hook on the wall.

4

The cool morning air blew against her makeup-free face when she opened the door. She inhaled the salty air, and watched the sun peaking over the horizon of the ocean. They calmed her nerves as she made her way down the stairs and to her car. Starting the engine, she pulled out of the parking lot and towards the hotel where Meredith, her mother, had worked before she was arrested for murdering the guests.

CHAPTER 2

Cars lined the two-lane street along the hotel. Clusters of people stood behind the police barricades, trying to get a glimpse behind them. PC Sanchez was directing traffic and attempting, without luck, to keep it moving smoothly so people could get to work.

Angel shook her head and got out of the car. The drawback of living on a small island: everybody knew your business whether you wanted them to or not. She took an evidence bag out of the truck. She'd stopped by the police station to get one.

Large Casuarina trees, like long bony fingers, loomed over the rundown single-story building, making it seem eerie and mysterious. The Galleon Bay had once been one of the leading hotels on the island—not five stars, but it had provided visitors with an enjoyable island experience. Now it was a forgotten dump where college kids stayed during spring breaks and summer vacation because of the cheap rates.

She ignored the dirty looks from the people PC Johnson attempted to keep behind the barricades. They were a continuous reminder that the years she'd spent off-island hadn't helped them forget her. What stories would be on the Marl Road today?

The scent of drunken debauchery lingered in the air as she entered the building. Scattered stains on the hallway carpet told stories of young visitors throwing up on it so often, no amount of cleaning could have removed the smells or stains. Closing her eyes, she braced emotionally for what awaited her down the long blue corridor.

This hotel had been her playground when she was a child, filled with happy memories, laughter, and Meredith scooping her up in her arms and hugging her tightly. She adjusted the weight of her evidence bag from one hand to the other as she remembered the joy in Meredith's eyes.

PC Ebanks stood outside room four, his large frame filling the narrow corridor and paunchy belly straining against his white uniform shirt.

"You working the scene?" he asked when he noticed the evidence bag.

"Yes. What's the story?"

"Front desk clerk found her dis mornin' when she didn't answer her six o'clock wake-up call," he said when she reached him.

All it took was one person to hear a bit of gossip and the whole island was texting and hanging around. "That explains the crowd. What about the guests?"

"Yeah, we told 'em to stay in their rooms and constables are posted at all the exits." Ebanks watched her with beady brown eyes, making her wonder if he was checking her out or waiting for her to do something crazy.

"Good. Nobody comes in until the EMTs get here."

His tanned jawline tightened and he glared at her as if saying he didn't need to be told how to do his job.

"Thanks." *Nice going, Angel. Just let him do his job.*

His aggravated stare burned the back of her neck even after the door closed behind her.

Death, sharp and pungent, stung her nose as she looked around to get her bearings. Placing her evidence bag on the floor, she put on latex gloves and started taking pictures, and visually checked the room for evidence. Nothing seemed out of the ordinary and there was no indication of there having been a struggle. The killer didn't bother to hide the fact that the victim wasn't alone before she died. Two wine glasses sat on the counter of the small kitchenette, one with lipstick and one without. She placed both glasses in evidence bags.

Angel liked to save her inspection of the body for last, after she'd gotten a good feel for the scene and what the killer may have been trying to say with the crime committed. As she got closer to the bed in the middle of the room, she saw that the victim was a white, middle-aged woman wearing only her bra and panties. Thick droplets of blood made tracks from her neck to just below her white bra. Her perfectly styled dark hair and makeup appeared undisturbed. Except for her neck, no other wounds were apparent.

She leaned over the body to take a closer look. Her hand froze when she reached the neck of the victim and noticed a roughly cut slash from one ear to the other. The marks looked similar to those on the bodies of Meredith's victims. Panic rose in her throat, closing off her air. The images of the victims and their dead bodies were branded in her mind. And not just from her study of the case photos...

Deep breaths, Angel.

She searched her thoughts frantically for memories after she had passed out the night before, but there was nothing. The chains, along with the deadbolt locks, had been secured this morning before she left the apartment—she had made sure.

With shaky hands, she continued to process around the body, wiping her own forehead more than once with the back of her sleeve to keep her sweat from dripping onto the scene. At the bottom edge of the bed, she picked up a strand of hair. She thought it was strange that there were no other strands from the victim anywhere else in the room. Angel looked at the strand closely. It was dark, like the victim's hair, but the texture appeared different. There was only one way to know for sure. If she was lucky, it belonged to the killer. She took a sample of the victim's hair and placed both in separate bags, labeling them carefully. She sealed the victim's hands in paper bags to ensure any evidence on them was preserved until the body reached the pathologist.

One thing that bothered her about the scene was how everything was meticulously placed, as if the killer had gone to great lengths for everything to be where it was, from the body to the glasses that were set so neatly next to each other. Everything was too perfect. Coupled with the similarities of the wound, uneasiness gripped her.

About ten minutes later, there was a soft knock on the door. "Ready for pickup?" the EMTs asked from the doorway.

"Yeah, come in." Thankfully, she'd stopped sweating and her hands weren't trembling as much.

"Well, she's definitely dead," one of them said after checking her pulse and other signs of life.

Two EMTs lifted the corpse into a black body bag on the stretcher they'd wheeled in.

"Let Jackson know I'll stop by the hospital later," she told them.

One of the EMTs nodded.

Angel looked around the hotel room one more time to make sure she'd checked everything before leaving.

"Have the staff been questioned?" she asked Ebanks on her way out.

He nodded. "I think so, but double-check with Johnson." He pulled up his uniform pants, which were falling precariously low.

"Thanks for keeping the others from coming in while I was working." She acknowledged her thanks with a nod of her head. It wasn't easy to keep investigators away from a murder scene, and one as significant as this one was a challenge.

He nodded and gave her a relaxed smile as he leaned against the doorway. Angel shook her head and she walked away. *Next thing you know, he'd be lighting up for a smoke.*

9

Ebanks was good at his job, but sometimes she felt he didn't take it seriously enough.

She made her way through the hotel, looking for other officers. She found Johnson trying to answer questions from a couple of nosy housekeeping staff standing by their cleaning cart. He towered over them by several inches, but as she got closer, she could see they'd backed him into a corner. His polite English demeanor was no match for them.

"Excuse us, ladies," she interrupted.

She almost smiled at the relief on his face. It was one thing to keep a pushy crowd at bay; it was another entirely to dodge questions of determined housekeepers who wanted the details of the excitement that happened at work.

"Have all the guests and staff been questioned?" she asked.

"Yes, with the exception of the bartender. Those ladies cornered me before I could get to him."

"Has the victim been identified?"

"Yes. An American woman, in her late forties. She arrived last week."

"I'll get the bartender. If he was working last night, he might have seen something."

Johnson didn't reply as he glanced nervously down the hallway, as if worried that the ladies he'd escaped earlier would jump out now that his conversation with Angel was over.

She headed to the green hallway she remembered led to the bar, and wondered if it still looked like the inside of a pirate ship. When she spotted a wood-paneled wall mounted with swords, which led to an entrance with sides made of knotted ropes, she got her answer. She headed into the bar and set her bag down. She took out her camera, and scanned through the photos until she reached a close-up with a clear view of the victim's face.

She knocked on the wooden top of the bar to get the

bartender's attention. When he turned around, deep ocean-blue eyes moved over her intently.

He set aside the glass in his hand as he leaned forward, rested his arms on the bar, and flashed a sexy grin. "What can I do for you, beautiful?"

Angel cringed. He was Irish. His accent reminded her too much of someone she'd been trying to forget. Not Irish, but close enough. "It's Inspector."

She placed her camera down on the bar so he could see the photo of the victim. "Was this woman here last night?"

Lean fingers picked up the camera. "Is that the murdered guest?"

"Yes. Was she here?"

"Aye."

"Was she alone?"

"No. A fella with long, dark hair was with her. Couldn't keep her hands off him." He grinned.

"What else can you tell me about him?"

He shrugged. "Didn't get a good look at him. It was dark."

"If it was so dark, how do you know it was the same woman?"

"I saw her come in earlier. She was older than the usual college students, but I didn't see them together until later when it was crowded. By then, it was just flashing dance lights."

"Did they leave together?" she asked, taking the camera off the counter.

"Couldn't say."

"Was his bill paid by credit card?"

"I'll check, but I don't think so. Don't remember any credit card transactions cashing out last night. Most students pay cash or charge the drinks to their room." Walking to the phone mounted on the wall, he spoke with someone for a brief moment before returning. "No credit card charges and the dead guest was the only room charge."

A frown creased her brow. The killer wasn't a tourist. She felt it in her gut. That, and that he was definitely familiar with Meredith's murders. She took notes on their discussion.

"Fancy a drink? Your face says you need one," he asked when he answered her final question.

Her eyes roamed over shoulders flexed against his tight-fitting 'I dive deep' T-shirt. "I'm on duty."

He leaned in closer and his voice lowered to a seductive tone. "I can keep a secret."

"I don't drink."

"How about something else from the bar?"

"Unless you have the name of the man who was with the victim last night, there's nothing you have that I want."

"Your lips are saying no, but your eyes, aye, tell a different story."

"And what do you think they're saying?"

"You're parched and want a drink, badly."

Oh, he was good. "Harassing an officer could land you behind bars."

"Will there be handcuffs first?"

Angel put her hands up to stop him from saying more. A woman was killed in the place he worked and he was flirting. *Seriously?* She made a mental note to look at his interview notes in detail.

"Here's my card," she said and dropped it on the counter, not wanting to risk him trying to touch her hand. She moved away from the bar. "Call me if you think of anything else."

"Can I call after hours?"

"If it's related to the case, yes."

"What if it's personal?"

Her hazel eyes held his blue ones firmly.

"That's a no then." He chuckled.

After getting contact details from the bartender, Jeff, she left the bar and headed to the parking lot. She groaned when she spotted Daniel Rumson, a reporter from Cayman Newsroom, standing behind the barricades, next to Sanchez.

"Has the victim been identified?" Daniel asked as she got closer.

She didn't answer.

"Is it just a coincidence that the murder occurred at the same hotel your mother killed her first victim, Ms. Mason?"

She squeezed the handle of her evidence bag. She hated being called by her last name. Everyone knew that, including him.

"It's Inspector," Sanchez corrected.

"Wasn't yesterday twenty years to the day that your mother was captured for killing five people, Inspector?" he stated in a condescending tone.

"Back off," Sanchez barked. He glared at Daniel, daring him to say another word.

The microphone in Daniel's hand dropped to his side and he took a step back.

Man, how she hated him. He'd done nothing but harass her with questions the moment he found out who she was. He was a midget next to Sanchez, but he didn't let that deter him from pushing the microphone towards her. He was a tenacious bulldog who didn't care what it took to get the news to the general public.

"The press will be contacted once we have more details," she said, and walked behind Sanchez, who moved Daniel and his cameraman out of the way so she could get to her car.

"Thanks."

Sanchez nodded and gave her a dazzling smile.

She got in her car and pulled away from the hotel, relieved to see it get smaller in her rearview mirror. All the constables knew her history; some had been just joining the force when Meredith had been captured. Most of them hadn't warmed up to her even after two years, but she preferred it that way. Sanchez started working within weeks of her, as well as Johnson. They, along with Ebanks, were the only constables who didn't shun her.

She put down the car window and let the breeze blow through the car, not caring about the humidity, but loving the smells of fruit trees from the small Caribbean house she passed.

Many things had changed in the twelve years she'd been gone: there were more buildings, more stores and fast-food restaurants, more shopping centers, and large fancy beach houses. But she knew if she took a turn down a back road or two, she'd still find old wooden houses with dirt or sand yards, with stray chickens and dogs running wild, along with a shirtless kid or two. She'd missed it, missed the clear water of the sea, its salty smell, and sandy beaches. Cayman was home in a way England never was.

She loved the stray chickens that wandered around downtown, and that vendors didn't haggle tourists on the street the way they did on other islands. She loved that children swam in the sea in their underwear across from waterfront stores that sold expensive jewelry and clothing.

She drove past the police station and headed towards the hospital, which was less than a mile from downtown. Although processing bodies wasn't her favorite part of the job, she was thankful for the distraction from the evidence that screamed this crime was similar to Meredith's case.

CHAPTER 3

As she strolled down the long, cream-colored corridors of the hospital, the photos of scenes from the islands hanging on the walls didn't lift her spirits the way they usually did. Her heart raced and her armpits were sweating again when she reached the morgue.

Two forensic staff chatted in the corner of the room, not bothering to look up when she entered. That was fine with her. She never bothered to ask anyone's names or make polite conversation. Finding out names meant having to make small talk, which led to more talking, and that could lead to caring. She liked it better this way, even if it meant them thinking she was stuck-up.

Jackson stood next to the body, studying it intently. Ebony strands clung to his head like a bad toupee and his skin looked like the belly of a frog—pale and slimy. His lab coat was always impeccably clean, which led her to believe he kept a secret stash of them somewhere—ready for him to change into at the first sign of a stain.

He looked up and gave her a slight smile, showing off his slight overbite. She took out her camera and walked up to the metal table where Jackson stood over the victim.

"Hey, Jackson."

He nodded his hello and pushed his thick-rimmed glasses farther onto his nose, his attention fixed on the body as he motioned one of the forensic staff to help him prop it up.

15

Angel stood on the metal step next to Jackson and started taking photos of the victim. She listened as he rattled off details for the forensic staff to record as the bra and panties were removed from the victim. She took pictures of the parts of the body she hadn't been able to at the scene. Her face seemed serene, as though she was merely sleeping.

"I hate this part," she whispered, last night's vodka binge churning in her stomach.

"Really? I thought you liked this part," he said, his voice heightening with excitement as his hands moved over the body, checking for wounds.

"Why would you think that?" She gave him a sideways glance. The only part she liked was finding out how the victim was killed, and if the killer left behind evidence she could use to put him behind bars.

"You find out how they died." He paused and looked up at her. "You get the interesting part of the job."

Her brows knotted.

"Discovering how it happened…" He inspected the marks on the victim's neck. "Looks like the mark of something with a very jagged edge." He wiped his forehead with the back of his glove-covered hand. "Hmm. I vaguely remember seeing this type of wound before, on another body. I can't recall which one. It'll come to me."

"It's similar to the victims in the Meredith Mason cases," she clarified.

No sense in beating around the bush. It would come out soon enough. He didn't bat an eye at the mention of Meredith's name. The forensic staff looked away when she glanced at them.

"Do you think it's a coincidence?" he asked as he continued to inspect the body.

"That's what I'm going to find out." Although the wounds appeared similar, she hoped it was a fluke. "Is the wound on her neck the cause of death?" she asked, peering over his head.

16

"Not sure yet, but it would appear so."

"Any signs of sexual assault?" Angel asked, taking pictures of the naked body.

"No." Jackson motioned for one of the forensic staff to assist him with turning over the body.

"Hmm…really?" Angel felt that this was strange as the victim was half naked, which implied the intent was there. But Angel knew there was no telling what went on in the mind of a killer and why they never did the obvious. "Email me the toxicology report once you get the results of what was in her system." She put her camera back in the bag and took out evidence containers.

She took samples from underneath the victim's fingernails, and then packaged them in the containers and tagged it. After recording the information she needed for the case, she mumbled her goodbyes to Jackson and his staff. She was thankful to leave the morgue and all its strange smells. She went the back way to get to the parking lot and her car so she wouldn't have to go through the main hospital again.

As Angel pulled into the parking lot of the police station, her stomach churned, and anxiety of what awaited her inside the building filled the small space of her car, closing around her until she couldn't breathe.

She rested her forehead on her arms, covering the steering wheel, and took deep breaths. Visions of the bloody flesh around the victim's neck replayed in her mind. She squeezed her eyes shut to try to block them out.

When her breathing and heartbeat returned to normal, she lifted her head and stared up at the Cayman Islands crest over the entrance of the three-story orange and blue building. She got out of the car, grabbed her evidence bag and walked through the outer blue entrance.

A flurry of noise greeted her when she got inside. Two people were speaking with the officer behind the glass window, one of them starting to raise their voice. A man, dark and dingy, sat in one of the chairs along the wall. His eyes were lit up like a Christmas tree and his mouth rattled nonsense. She spotted the handcuffs when she saw an officer standing next to him telling him to keep quiet. No one noticed her as she swiped her card to the secondary entrance and headed to her office.

The voices from the other room dimmed the closer she got to her office and were overtaken by the chatting of the officers in the lunchroom, and their offices. The conversation slowed and then shrunk as she passed them. She ignored their penetrating stares and murmuring.

They would suspect her. It didn't matter that she wasn't even ten when Meredith was arrested. She didn't care. She had learned not to care a long time ago.

She kicked open her office door and spread the collected evidence out on the long table against the wall and next to her desk. Boxes, although neatly stacked, filled the remaining space along with filing cabinets.

Moments later, there was a knock on her office door. "Come in."

Sanchez swaggered in, shut the door behind him, and leaned against it as a frown creased his tanned, chiseled face.

She swallowed a groan. He was still at the scene when she left and she had hoped to avoid him completely today.

"How you holding up, Inspector Angel?"

Most everyone on the force called her by her first name. The CS called her Inspector Mason, but everyone else knew she didn't like them using her last name. It wasn't normal procedure, but the constables went along with it. "I'm fine."

"If you need someone to talk to…"

"I said I'm fine." His gesture would be sweet, but she knew it came with ulterior motives.

"Maybe I could take you out for a drink later. Get your mind off things."

And there it was. "I don't drink," she replied, sorting through the files on her desk.

"How about lunch?" he pressed.

Her eyes snapped to his face, not bothering to hide her impatience. It was a dance they had done at least once a month since she started, and one she'd hoped he'd end after her repeated refusals. Not to mention it was against regulations for fellow constables to date. That didn't seem to matter to him.

Soft brown eyes met hers and a smile curled his lips, making him more attractive, if that was possible. She'd initially been flattered by his attention, and glad that someone didn't look at her like she had a disease, like most of the other officers. She'd returned a few of his smiles and shared polite conversation, but she quickly learned there was nothing more to him than a pretty face. Getting involved with him, with anyone, would be a bad idea and not just because they worked together. What if he wanted to stay the night?

"I'm just trying to help."

The soft tone of his voice washed over her, surprising her. It still amazed her that he had no accent, despite being from Honduras.

"Thanks, but I don't need your help." She headed behind her desk to put some distance between herself and Sanchez. "Dismissed."

He stood by the door, staring at her like she was a dessert for him to eat.

She took a frustrated breath. "I'm your superior officer, Sanchez. Don't ever forget that," she said, her tone implying this was the last conversation she wanted to have about this. She met him with a steely gaze and he took a step back.

She went to her office door, opened it, and waited for him to leave. Some of the male constables didn't take the women on the force seriously. She'd spent several years on the London force and had to deal with all kinds, but she'd kept her head down and blended in with the other constables while she got the experience she wanted under her belt.

As she went back to review the photos and evidence on her table, memories of last night's horrific dream flooded her thoughts. The dream she'd had of her killing someone was so intense and clear that the metallic smell of blood had remained even after she woke up.

Dread descended on her. Had she blacked out and left her apartment last night? *No. It wasn't possible.* She'd bolted herself inside. She vowed to stop drinking even if it meant enduring the voices in her head.

Focus, Angel!

She pulled the hair and other items she'd processed at the scene for DNA analysis. She logged the details of the hair sample and placed it on her desk. It would take a couple of days to find out what she needed to know.

If the hair found at the scene was hers.

Her office phone rang. It was Chief Superintendent Williams.

"Inspector Angel."

"My office, ten minutes."

She cringed at his tone. Although he treated her professionally, she knew he didn't like her. The police commissioner had gone over his head to hire her for her position and she was certain he resented her for it. She couldn't fault him; she didn't like him either.

When she entered the CS's office, she noticed Johnson, Ebanks, and Sanchez were there. Four pairs of eyes settled on her.

Johnson's square shoulders grew as stiff as his cropped sandy hair. Sanchez avoided her gaze completely, which didn't surprise her after their last encounter. Ebanks adjusted his large frame in the chair and gave her his carefree islander smile.

"I want all of you overseeing this case. Inspector Mason, you're the lead. For the moment," Williams stated.

What the hell did "for the moment" mean? Alarms were

going off in her head, but she nodded curtly and shifted from one foot to the other. She was grateful it was these constables and not any of the others who didn't like her. They'd worked on cases together before, so it was nothing new, but this case had an added sense of tension none of them seemed to be comfortable with.

"Get to work," Williams ordered, sitting upright in his chair. "I want a status report as soon as possible."

Johnson, Ebanks, and Sanchez followed Angel out of Williams' office and closed the door behind them. She turned to face them.

"Johnson, you deal with the MIR. Ebanks, you compile the statements collected from the guests and staff from the hotel, and Sanchez, you talk to the press officer and see if we can contain what's shared with the press. I'll contact the victim's family. Let's meet in the MIR in two hours."

Each man nodded.

It was going to be a long day.

CHAPTER 4

Two days later, Angel stared at the results of the owner of the hair sample. It wasn't hers, but she'd hoped it was the killer's, or even the victim's. Her hope had been foolish. It should've been obvious from the meticulous scene that the killer was too smart to get caught this early in the game by leaving something as basic as a hair behind.

Hands shaking, she looked at the results again, secretly praying that they would change and that the recent events had put a strain on her eyesight. It wasn't a mistake.

Angel leaned back slowly in her chair. This was going to take this case to more places than she and anyone else would like.

There was a knock on her door.

"Come in."

Jackson strolled in. "Are you busy?"

She reasoned that the verdict must be bad if he had ventured to the station instead of calling her. His body language screamed discomfort.

"Now's good."

"I identified the weapon used," he said, and looked down at his feet.

"What do you mean you identified the weapon?"

The police usually identified possible weapons used, not the pathologist. Angel waited patiently for him to give her his answer and maybe even an explanation.

"It's a bread knife."

Her heartbeat jolted. *The same weapon Meredith had used on her victims.* This escalated the case considerably. Angel was already on pins and needles about having to tell CS Williams about the hair; this was bound to give him a conniption. "Are you certain?"

He nodded. "I tested it for myself." He shifted from one foot to the other. "When you mentioned the wounds were similar to your mother's case, I thought you might want to know before anyone else. Also, Rohypnol was in the victim's system, same as your mother's victims."

"Does anyone else know?"

He shook his head.

She didn't consider their relationship a "friendship" but they did have a mutual professional respect for each other. She knew she could count on him. "Good. I need a favor, Jackson."

"Name it," he said without hesitation.

"Please keep this between us. I need time to talk to CS Williams about this." She placed a hand on his shoulder, something she never did. "Thanks, Jackson. I really appreciate it."

He gulped and nodded. He looked at his watch. "I gotta go."

Before she could say more, he was out the door, leaving her to ponder what this new development would mean for her and the case.

She headed to CS Williams' office after confirming he was available. His deep voice beckoned her inside when she knocked on his door. A solemn expression met her and she noticed lines of fatigue around his eyes. She wasn't the only one losing sleep.

"What is it, Inspector Mason?" he asked.

"I just got the results from the hair sample found on the scene."

He looked up with expectant eyes filled with a glimmering hope that made her regret she had to crush them.

"It's Meredith Mason's."

Surprise and frustration rippled across his smooth, aging face. He swore under his breath before leaning back in his chair.

"There's more. The victim's wounds were made with the same weapon as those in Meredith Mason's murders, and the same drug was used." She spilled the last part quickly, thinking it wouldn't be as shocking.

His dark skin lightened two shades, and fear crept across his taut face as his eyes rested on her. "It could mean we have a copycat." He rubbed his temples. "If the press gets a hold of this…" he mumbled.

"I haven't shared it with anyone yet, but we can't keep it secret for long."

"Any other evidence?" Williams asked.

Angel paused. "None."

She decided not to mention her conversation with Jackson, at least not yet. Jackson was discrete and wouldn't leak information.

"No one gets wind of this, not even Johnson, Ebanks, or Sanchez. Not yet." He regarded her firmly for emphasis.

She kept her expression solemn, though she wondered why Williams wanted her to keep the information to herself. Constables had been known to talk to the press or leak information, but the constables he mentioned didn't strike her as the type. "I'll stall them as long as I can, but at some point they'll need to know."

"We'll handle it when the time comes," he assured her.

"Yes, sir."

"I want you to interview Meredith Mason." It was said so casually, as if he'd just asked her to handle a traffic violation.

"Excuse me?" He couldn't be serious.

"You heard me." His cool caramel eyes met hers,

unwavering. "If I send someone else, she won't talk."

He was part of the original investigation, so he knew her connection to Meredith. That also meant he knew her history with Meredith.

"I don't know her."

It wasn't a complete lie. She didn't think anyone knew Meredith, not even Meredith.

"You know her better than anyone and you're a good investigator," he countered.

"Are you certain this is a good idea, sir?" Her mouth was dry and her stomach as unsettled as a boat in rough weather.

"Let me worry about that. I want you to concentrate on doing what you do best, evidence and investigating. Oh, and for the meantime, also keep this to yourself."

Great. More secrets. "Sure."

He spun in his chair, giving her his back. She took it as her cue to leave and headed back to her office.

Turmoil churned the butterflies in her stomach at the thought of seeing and talking to Meredith again. She was eighteen the first and last time she had visited Meredith, and she was certain this time would be as bad as the last one.

CHAPTER 5

The next day, Angel entered CS Williams' office and her heartbeat stuttered. She saw a head of hair that at first glance appeared dark brown, but she knew hidden in its tamarind depths were streaks of rich auburn.

The hair on her arms stood to attention when the man turned to show the side view of his face. Long-forgotten goose bumps spread across her skin until they made her skin ache.

"Inspector Mason, this is Professor Bren MacDougal." He gestured for her to take a seat. "He's a criminal psychologist who's teaching at the local university and will be acting as a consultant on this case."

"Hello, Angel." His Scottish brogue flowed over her like warm whisky, tingling right down to her toes. *God, he looked good. Even better than he had in college. How was that possible?*

"You two know each other?" Williams' brow narrowed in obvious displeasure.

"Yes, we went to college together," Angel answered.

"Hmm. Small world," Williams mumbled.

"Aye, isn't it?" Bren agreed. His aqua eyes caressed her face.

The CS's brows furrowed as if contemplating his next comment.

"We were lab partners," Angel said, looking pointedly at Williams. The last thing she wanted him thinking was that there'd been something between her and Bren.

"I see," Williams said, and visibly relaxed. "Professor MacDougal will be assisting with the unidentified subject's profile and anything else he can help with." Williams laced his fingers together. "We need all the expertise we can get."

She wanted to say they didn't need his help, but that would have been a lie.

Angel could feel Bren's stare burning her skin, but she didn't look at him at first. It had been eight years since she'd seen him and she needed more time to get her emotions under control.

"Welcome to the team," she said when her eyes finally met his.

"Thank you," Bren replied, his tone formal.

"He'll also be accompanying you on your trip to see Meredith." Williams glanced back and forth between them. "He can provide insight to Meredith's responses and reactions."

Bren had been one of the best criminal psychologists at Cambridge, so why was he here, in Cayman? She didn't know. She hadn't followed his career, afraid a connection of any kind would make her miss him.

"Sure," Angel said through gritted teeth. What she really wanted to say was "Hell no!"

"You can show me the pictures of the scene so I can look over them. When the other evidence is done, we can evaluate it again to see if we missed anything," Bren said in a professional tone.

A thin smile pulled at her lips. It was the same line she'd given him the first day they had become lab partners, only he hadn't been as confident then.

"Good. It's settled. You two work on the profile, speak with Meredith, and bring the rest of the team up to speed."

Williams spoke with assurance, as if he was certain they'd provide information to bring in the suspect. He was months away from retiring, but she knew he wouldn't leave with an open murder case.

"Stay a minute, Inspector Mason. It won't take long," Williams said.

Bren stood. "Take your time. I'll be outside, and then you can take me to your office."

She didn't get a chance to respond. He was out the door, the etched glass all but slammed in her face. The tension in the building was about to reach full capacity. As if things weren't bad enough, now Bren would be trying to psychoanalyze her like he had in college. *Just great!*

"Did you two have a relationship?" Williams asked bluntly.

Normally she'd say it was none of his business, but their working relationship begged the question. "No. We were lab partners and little more than friends."

"Good." He visibly relaxed.

What would he have done if she told him the truth? It didn't matter. It had nothing to do with the case and happened a long time ago.

"Send Professor MacDougal back in. We didn't finish. You can have him when I'm done."

That was the problem. She didn't want him. Him miles away was what she wanted. "Sure."

The impression of the door handle branded her palm when she closed it behind her. She headed back to her office, anxiety pressing down on her until the ceiling and walls seemed to close in on her.

The time that had elapsed since she'd last seen him disappeared and every emotion she'd suppressed during their time apart flooded to the surface in crashing waves. As she opened the door to her office, she prayed the intensity of her memories didn't reflect in her eyes.

"Fancy seeing you here." His voice dropped an octave.

These were the same words he'd said to her their last

night together. She swallowed deeply to regain her composure. "CS Williams wants to speak with you."

He closed the space between them faster than she could move away. Moving wasn't an easy task in her already crammed office.

"Still as organized as ever, I see," he said, as if it wasn't a good thing.

She tilted her chin, hating that she had to look up at him. She folded her arms over her chest to keep him at a distance, and to try to keep herself from hearing the thundering of her heart that echoed in her ears. "I like being organized."

A playful grin tugged the corners of his mouth. "I'll be back. Don't disappear on me," he quipped, his words hinting that he hadn't forgotten the fact she'd left college without saying goodbye.

She stepped away from the door, giving him space to leave.

The breath she was holding came out in a whoosh when the door closed behind him. She went over to the table, trying to block out the memory of their one and only night together—especially the voices and nightmare of her slitting Bren's throat while Meredith stood by with an evil grin, nodding her approval.

CHAPTER 6

Bren looked at the man sitting behind the desk and wondered if he'd misunderstood him. "Excuse me?"

"I want you to assess Inspector Mason," he repeated.

When he'd received the phone call hours earlier, requesting his help with the profile, this was the last thing he'd expected. *Was this Williams' original reason for asking him to join the investigation?*

"Why?"

CS Williams cupped his chin in his hand, his expression indicating his hesitation in how much he wanted to share. "I want to make sure this case doesn't affect her ability to do her job or her emotional stability."

"Has she shown signs of instability?" Bren asked. He didn't mention she'd worked in the UK for several years dealing with murder cases; Williams likely knew this. Besides, it would imply he knew more about her than he should.

"So far, no. But she keeps to herself a little more than most."

Bren relaxed. Studying Angel would be interesting, but he'd rather they didn't start their working relationship that way. "It's understandable, given her history."

"She told you about it?" Williams' eyebrows rose in surprise.

"No." Bren could count on one hand how many times Angel told him something personal about herself in the four years they'd known each other. "I read newspaper articles for a class. She was very young at the time. That would damage any ten-year-old's psyche."

"I don't want to take the chance of her cracking under the stress of this case and do something out of character," Williams said carefully.

She was a suspect. Was that another reason he was asked to help with the profile? Did Williams think Angel would fit it? It had crossed his mind too, given her family history, but only for a brief moment. It was not the norm for children of serial killers to become killers themselves. Besides, Angel prided herself on being in control of every aspect of her life, including her emotions. He knew that better than anyone.

Seeing her today had brought back memories, good and bad. She was still as beautiful as ever, although her hair was longer. Part Indian, part Caribbean, she looked nothing like the other students at college. It had made her unique and more stunning. If Angel was going to be psychoanalyzed by anyone, it was going to be him, someone she once considered a friend.

"I'll do it."

Williams moved his chair to a more upright position. "Is your past relationship going to be a problem?"

Bren's heart stopped. *How did he know?* He was certain Angel wouldn't have told him. He rationalized: he must have meant going to college together. "No."

Williams stood up and extended his hand for Bren to shake. "Good. She said you were merely acquaintances, but I had to be sure."

Acquaintances! The word was a bitter taste in his mouth.

"Have Angel show you around," Williams said before turning his attention back to his computer.

He told himself he was helping Angel, but even as he shook Williams' hand and left his office, he couldn't help feeling he was betraying her in some small way.

He headed to Angel's office and found her seated behind her desk.

"CS Williams suggested you introduce me to the officers I'll be working with." Bren tried not to make it sound like an order. She wasn't happy about his presence, that much was clear from her body language in Williams' office.

She pushed her chair away from her desk, stood up, and headed towards him. "Let's get this over with," he heard her mumble.

Bren held the door open for her and followed her through the surprisingly quiet station. She passed several officers before entering a room.

"This is the MIR—Major Evidence Room." Angel didn't pause to explain what everything in the room was for, but headed straight to the far end where two men sat. One was obviously a local with his tan skin, relaxed full frame, and casual smile. The other's back was straight as a rod with hair to match. Two pairs of eyes sized him up.

"Johnson, Ebanks. This is Bren MacDougal. He's a criminal psychologist and will be helping with the murder case at the Galleon Bay."

They both looked at each other before looking at him. Neither seemed pleased to see him. Johnson was the first to stand up and extend his hand in welcome.

Bren shook Johnson's hand and expected him to say something, but he just gave a quick nod and sat back down.

Several seconds passed before Bren realized PC Ebanks wasn't going to extend the same courtesy so he made the gesture. Thankfully, Ebanks shook his hand, but like Johnson, he remained silent.

"This room is where we'll spend most of our time, other than my office."

"Where will I be? Here or in your office?"

Her face crunched in discomfort and then what appeared to be thought. "You'll be sharing my office for the moment."

Word must have gotten out, because soon the room filled with more constables. Angel introduced him, and he shook their hands readily or acknowledged their nods and threw in an occasional "I look forward to working with you," for good measure.

Angel rushed through the explanation of the room's contents, their purpose, and who was responsible for what. He was grateful to learn PC Johnson was in charge of the room. It was easier than trying to recall the names of several people.

He followed Angel out of the MIR and back to her office but not before stopping to show him the kitchen and the coffee pot. From the state of the pot, stained from old coffee, he decided he would be stopping at the coffee shop instead.

Her back was stiff and her frosty demeanor remained throughout the rest of the tour, but from the expressions on the officer's faces, it wasn't anything out of the ordinary. They seemed more interested in him, and he felt their eyes follow him back to Angel's office.

"What are you doing here, Bren?" she asked bluntly when she closed the door.

"I'm here to help."

"Here, in Cayman," she clarified.

"I'm teaching at the law school."

He didn't miss the shock in her eyes. "Why would the CS ask you to help?"

He shrugged. "We're acquainted through mutual friends and he knows my background. He thought the police could use my help." *Did she suspect the other reason CS Williams wanted him here?*

Her spine straightened. "Just remember you're here to consult, not lead. Got it?"

He strode up to her desk and placed his hands on the

surface, leaning so close she couldn't avoid his scrutiny. "As long as you get that I'm here to help, Angel." The tangy smell of sea and salt drifted to his nose and he had the urge to take a strand of her hair and get a better whiff.

She pushed her chair away from the desk, putting distance between them. "Good. Once we understand each other."

"I understand perfectly." He glanced over her neck to her ears and then her full glossy lips. They shimmered invitingly. He pushed himself upright. *Not good, Bren!*

"Is our past relationship going to be an issue for you?" she asked, interrupting his thoughts.

"No," he answered too quickly.

"Good."

Her cold tone stung him, but the case was more important than what happened between them all those years ago. She'd left him without a fare-thee-well and he had no intention of letting her get under his skin again.

CHAPTER 7

The next morning, Angel was on edge from the voices she hadn't been able to drown out with alcohol, which was making her second-guess her decision not to drink. She'd gotten three hours of sleep, if that.

As she walked through the front door of the police station, she prayed the eyedrops she'd put in earlier and the strong coffee in her hand would take her through the day.

Bren's wide shoulders were the first thing she noticed when she entered her office. *How the hell had he gotten in?* She'd steeled herself against seeing him this morning, but nothing had prepared her for her heart jerking or stomach flipping at the sight of him sitting at the chair by her desk.

He was confident now and as gorgeous as ever. Things had obviously gotten better for him. She hadn't been so lucky. Since college, the nightmares and voices had gotten worse. She was never able to tell him. She hadn't wanted to be psychoanalyzed by the man she was falling in love with.

He smiled when he saw her and held out a coffee for her. "Caramel macchiato, right?"

Did he remember everything about her? She didn't know whether to be flattered or annoyed. "It's plain coffee these days," she replied, holding up her own cup. "Let's get started." She grabbed a pen and notepad from her desk with her free hand. "Let's hit the MIR."

Bren followed her out of the office.

She nodded to the constables they passed in the hallways while Bren greeted each with a "good morning" or "how's it going?".

Johnson was already in the MIR when they arrived. He gave them a nod of his sandy head when they entered.

"This case has similarities to another, so I thought we'd look at both side by side." She pointed to the signs she'd made with the dates of when the murders had occurred. "So, what do you think?"

"I think you've got a nut case on your hands," Bren replied without even looking at all the evidence.

She gave him a sideways glance. "Is that your professional opinion?"

He grinned, flashing perfect teeth under kissable lips. "The subject has homicidal tendencies, which he takes out on his fellow human beings."

He stepped closer until she could smell the scent of his cologne. It was the same one he had worn in college; the same one that remained in her hair and on her clothes after they'd made love.

"Hmm, the victims were placed in the same position and the wounds the killer inflicted are the same as the first case. The only difference is their sex. Were there any signs of sexual assault?" Bren asked.

"No," Angel replied.

"Really? Interesting." He glanced over the photos of both scenes once more, this time slower. "What about the first case?"

"No. She lured them with the promise of sex, but never went through with it." Angel took a small step to distance herself from him and the scent of his cologne.

"Was that in the case files?"

She nodded.

He stepped back from the wall, and glanced over the

photos again, as if checking for something he missed. "It appears the killer is extremely thorough."

"Why would anyone want to replicate a murder?"

He shrugged. "There could be several reasons. They wanted to impress the first killer, or they simply admired their work and wanted to duplicate it."

"But Meredith is no longer on the island. She's been in England the past twenty years."

"They could send letters, pictures, anything to let her know what they'd done," he reasoned.

Had the killer sent something to Meredith? She scribbled on her notepad.

"Why was she sent to England instead of remaining here?" Bren asked.

"Cayman doesn't have facilities for criminals with mental disorders, especially those who were as dangerous as Meredith." The politicians had wanted to remove her completely from the island to show the public they'd taken care of the situation. Out of sight, out of mind.

"Makes sense," he said with a shrug.

He turned to face her. "Are we going to ignore the giant elephant in the room?" Bren said softly.

"What do you mean?" She kept her eyes on what she'd just written. *Seriously? He was going to bring that up now?* Thankfully, he had whispered so the constables on the other side of the room didn't hear him.

"Well, the last time we saw each other was eight years ago, and you left school without saying goodbye."

She was glad he didn't say it was the morning after they'd made love. "I didn't think it was relevant to the case," she said coolly in a low tone.

He shrugged as if he didn't care. "It's not. I just thought we should clear the air, but I see it isn't necessary." His tone was emotionless.

She couldn't afford to lose control like Meredith had.

"Do you have any other questions?"

"Aye." His intense aqua eyes held hers and she looked away quickly, her heart racing. "But they have nothing to do with the case, so I'll hold them for later." He cleared his throat and turned his attention back to the pictures on the wall.

"We should look at Meredith: her motives and how she chose her victims. It might help, especially if her murders are being replicated." Bren took a seat at the table where the case files were stacked.

"Okay," she said tentatively. Digging into Meredith's memories and head was the last thing she wanted to do with him. She pulled out the file with the statements and placed them before him.

"We know she chose men, always tourists, between their mid-twenties and thirties. This killer's first victim was middle-aged, but twenty years have passed, so maybe the suspect is taking that into consideration, or is older," Bren observed before continuing. "Four weeks passed between each murder, and if this suspect is copying the murders exactly, we could have that long."

She let out the breath she didn't realize she was holding. Having a month to find the suspect gave her some relief, but not much. For all they knew, the killer could be on a plane back to wherever he lived.

***

As their conversation progressed, Bren waited patiently for her to tell him something about her mother, but she didn't. CS Williams' concerns were valid, but he still held on to the opinion that her having a sense of control was too important. The real question was if her need for that control would cause her to snap under too much pressure.

"They enjoy inflicting pain; that is evident in the use of the jagged weapon. They like to be in control. The victim wasn't bound to keep them from resisting, which could mean the victim was weaker and didn't need to be subdued." He flipped through a few pages. "How did the subject from the first case subdue her victims?"

"She drugged them."

"Was the same drug used for this victim?"

"Yes."

"Hmm." He rested his hand against the side of his head.

"There weren't signs of a struggle at the scene, but this killer is meticulous and might have straightened up to give the appearance he wanted."

"Or she," he corrected. He studied her as she digested his words.

"What?"

"Ye said he. The killer could be a woman," he clarified.

"If the killer was a woman, wouldn't she choose men as her victims as Meredith had?" she reasoned.

"Maybe. Or the killing might have nothing to do with Meredith. The killer could be using her case and female victims to hide the fact she's a woman."

She looked at the photos of the scene again. "But the bartender said he saw the victim with a man."

"Did he see them leave together?" Bren asked.

"No, but what about the lipstick-free glass in the room?"

"Not every woman wears lipstick when they go out," Bren said. Angel never had, but he didn't mention that. Her lips were pulled in a thin line, an indication she was getting agitated.

"Now you're just grasping at straws!" Her raised tone caught the attention of other constables in the room. She turned her back to them and pretended to review the file in front of her.

"We should pull the files on all the original victims. If the killer is a copycat, it might give us an idea where they'll strike next." He closed the open file before him and pushed it aside.

39

She pointed to a stack of files. "That's all of them."

"What about the personal statements of the...witnesses?" He chose the words carefully and kept his attention on the other evidence, as though he was carefully studying it.

"They are all in the file."

"Good." He finally raised his head and gave her a friendly smile.

After shifting through the files on the table, she pulled out a folder. "My statement is in here. You can analyze it to your heart's content, Bren," she said snidely.

He took it from her hand. "That's not what I was looking for."

"Oh, then what?" She put her hands on her hips in annoyance.

"The psychiatric assessments."

One hand dropped from her hip. "Of Meredith or me?"

"You call your mother Meredith?"

It was something he'd noticed earlier and figured it was because she thought he didn't know Meredith was her mother, or to keep their conversation professional. But when she didn't slip once, his curiosity was piqued.

Another constable sauntered over before she could answer him. He stopped short when he saw Bren. He didn't hide his surprise or displeasure before he covered it with a crisp smile.

"Bren, this is PC Sanchez." She gestured between them with her hand. "Bren is helping with the case."

"You're the shrink," Sanchez stated, taking a step closer to Angel.

Bren's back straightened and he lowered his rejected hand. "Criminal psychologist," he clarified. *Who was this jackass?*

"Right. You free for lunch, Inspector?" he asked Angel, dismissing Bren.

Bren felt the primal urge to grab Sanchez by the collar.

40

To throw him and his perfect hair and smile to the ground and pound the shit out of him.

"No," she replied coolly, making Bren wonder if it was because he was there.

"We can meet again after lunch," Bren said politely.

"Agreed. Back here in an hour and a half?" Angel suggested.

Bren suppressed the urge to give Sanchez a smug, triumphant look. "Sure."

A morgue-like silence hung in the air before Bren headed to the door.

"Are we still on for tonight?" he heard Sanchez ask as he left the MIR.

He walked past the clutter of desks and through the metal front door of the station. It was only when he reached his car that he relaxed.

Bren started the engine. Sanchez mentioned them meeting at night. *Did that mean they were dating?* It didn't matter to him. He was there to help profile the killer and provide a psychological assessment of Angel. Nothing more. He longed to punch his hand through the windshield and imagine it was Sanchez's face, but instead he shifted gears and pulled out of the crowded parking lot and into the road.

CHAPTER 8

"You want me to what?"

"I want you to speak with the press."

Angel looked across the desk at Williams. *He couldn't be serious?* She was the last person to speak with the press.

"You heard me."

"Sir, shouldn't the press officer handle it?" That was the usual procedure, so why was she doing it?

"Normally yes, but we don't have much choice. The police commissioner is breathing down my neck and the public and press are breathing down his. If we make a statement, it will keep the rumors under control."

"Especially if they're made by me, the daughter of the previously caught killer. Is that it?" She felt like the goat being put out to slaughter.

"Exactly."

"Do I take them through the MIR?" she asked, knowing there was no use trying to talk him out of it. He'd given an order and she would respect it, even if she didn't like or agree with it.

"Not this time."

She took a calming breath. "Okay, who am I speaking with?"

"Daniel Rumson from Cayman Newsroom."

Ah hell! She was afraid he'd say that.

"I'm very serious," Williams answered. "You're meeting with him at two this afternoon."

She gritted her teeth. She really didn't want to do this. "Will that be all, sir?"

"Dismissed."

Two o'clock came faster than she liked and before she knew it, she, Sanchez, and Johnson were standing outside the station. At least she wasn't alone. She didn't know why Sanchez was there, but she knew Johnson was there to step in and keep the peace if things got out of hand. He always kept a cool head. She indulged the image of Sanchez knocking Daniel down in the parking lot of the police station. Now that would be news!

He met them outside the station in the parking lot. They stood for several minutes while Daniel and his cameraman got their equipment and picked a spot to set up. More than once Johnson checked his watch and Sanchez adjusted the collar of the shirt underneath his uniform.

"Be thankful they changed from polyester a few years ago, Sanchez," she said.

"Polyester in the Caribbean sun and humidity?" His gaze moved to Johnson, who nodded to confirm it wasn't a joke.

She used to joke that's why the constables looked so miserable. Who wouldn't be in a polyester uniform patrolling in ninety-five degree weather without a lick of breeze?

"Are you almost ready, Daniel?" What she really wanted to ask was how long did it take to set up one lousy camera? If they were looking for a shot, they could do it after they were done talking.

"Almost," he replied, but made no move to hurry.

"We have places to be, Daniel, so if you can't take the shot now we'll have to reschedule for another time," she insisted.

That got his attention. He ran his fingers confidently through his neat sandy-colored hair and headed towards her. Being near him made her skin crawl as she remembered the way he'd harassed her when she returned to the island. He was worse than the reporters in the UK, and it wasn't just because his questions were personal or about a random case she was working on.

She shifted from one foot to the other, trying to get into a comfortable position. As Daniel gave his intro, she was thankful she didn't have to wear her hat. Sweat would be pouring down her face while she was on camera.

"I'm outside the police station, speaking with the officers on the case of the murder that occurred at the Galleon Bay hotel almost two weeks ago. With me is Inspector Angel Mason. Afternoon, Inspector."

"Good afternoon, Daniel."

"Can you tell us about the murder and what's being done to find the killer?"

"We've identified the victim, who was a visitor to the island, and have notified the family. The rest is still under investigation, Daniel."

"Is it true this murder is similar to the Meredith Mason case from twenty years ago?"

"We're still reviewing all the evidence."

Daniel paused for a moment too long, as if contemplating his next question. Panic, sharp and dark, pricked her.

"Is it possible a member of her family is responsible?" Daniel continued.

Rat bastard! "As I said, we're still investigating."

"You're related to Meredith Mason, right? Can you tell us why anyone would want to start the killings again?"

The image of her fist hitting his face flashed before her, but instead she replied calmly. "We can't say for sure, but we're doing everything we can to find out the truth."

"Has anyone in her family been questioned?" he pressed.

In her mind, she now kneed him in the groin, and when he doubled over, rammed his face with her knee, leaving him in the fetal position in the parking lot and shaking the dust from her shoes. It was a delightful scene in her mind. *Yes!*

Yes! Do it! Do it! came a voice in her head, followed by cackling laughter.

She said, "They're not suspects at the moment." She hoped to God her expression was as calm as her voice sounded. She pushed aside the voices. *Not now!*

"Why haven't they been questioned?" His green eyes held hers firmly, contradicting the friendly expression on his face.

Sanchez came up beside her. "We're focusing on all possible suspects at the moment and will continue to keep the press informed as the investigation progresses."

"Professor MacDougal is helping with profiling. Is that correct?" Daniel asked, now shifting to another topic.

About damn time!

"Yes, that's correct," she replied.

"Is your past relationship with him going to affect the investigation?"

Try as she might, Angel couldn't stop her reaction. Thankfully, neither could Sanchez or Johnson. She heard them curse under their breaths.

"Professor MacDougal and I were lab partners in college, which has nothing to do with the murder investigation."

"I heard you were more than lab partners."

His friendly expression was gone now that the camera was focused on her, as if primed for a reaction from her on live TV.

She lifted her chin, cracked two knuckles, and took a step towards him.

Johnson must have sensed her discomfort because he interceded. "That will be all for today."

It was a dismissal and one she'd never been more thankful for.

Daniel gave her a greasy smile that appeared to say "I got you." She hadn't liked him before today, but after what just happened, his name would top her hit list, if she had one.

They headed back into the station and left Daniel and his cameraman outside to take their final shots. She resisted the urge to have a constable tell him they couldn't stay because they were interfering with police business. It would be an outright lie and one she'd get crap for.

"Be grateful he didn't ask why you were on the case or mention that you're Meredith's daughter," Johnson said when they passed through the secondary doors.

"I suppose." He was right. As bad as it was, it could've been worse. Daniel's interviews were usually interrogations with little respect for privacy.

Johnson went back to his desk, but to her dismay, Sanchez followed her to the lunchroom. Unfortunately, no one else was there.

"Is it true?"

His brown eyes searched her, but she avoided them and opened a drawer to get a spoon. "Is what true?"

"That you and the professor were an item?"

"An item? What are we, in high school?" She smirked, and shook her head in annoyance.

Sanchez crossed his arms, appearing to try to make his chest appear broader than it really was and leaned his hip against the white counter.

"It's like I said. We were lab partners."

"Nothing more?" he pressed.

She reached into one of the overhead cabinets and took out a coffee mug. She didn't like lying, but she wasn't about to talk about her history with Bren, especially with Sanchez.

"We were also study buddies." That was an understatement. "Not that it's anyone's business."

Sanchez visibly relaxed, as if her answer would make or break the rest of his day.

He poured her a cup of coffee and gave her his "stop you dead in your tracks" smile, one she was certain worked with every woman who crossed his path, including other female constables.

He'd taken a step to close the already small space between them when Johnson burst through the door.

"CS wants a word with you, Inspector." He looked at Angel and then Sanchez. "That professor is with him."

Sanchez's gaze moved to her face. She nodded her reply.

She followed closely behind Johnson. When she reached Williams' office, she knocked and strode inside. Bren was sitting in one of the chairs.

"Have a seat." Williams motioned to the chair next to Bren.

Before her butt even had time to hit the chair, he declared, "You and Bren will be on the next plane to England to visit Meredith Mason."

This day was just getting better and better. *First her encounter with Daniel and now this?* The thought of being alone with Bren made her stomach do flips and the idea of seeing Meredith made it want to upchuck the jerk chicken sandwich she'd had earlier for lunch.

"How is she going to help?" Angel asked. Even though he'd said days ago she would be going, part of her had hoped something would change his mind or more evidence would present itself that wouldn't require making the trip.

"The copycat killer might have visited her, and she could describe him," Williams answered.

"Couldn't we save the government's money and talk to her over the phone?"

"No," Williams insisted. "And since when are you interested in saving the government money?"

She opened her mouth to argue, but knew it wasn't the best idea, especially with Bren there.

"Bren will help with accessing Meredith and her responses. I'm hoping between the two of you, you'll be able to get what we need to help with the case. Speak with the superintendent of the institution and let him know you're coming. Meredith's break between murders was a month, so we can't afford for this to drag out any longer."

Angel nodded. Bren was stone silent next to her. *What was he thinking? Was he salivating at the thought of interviewing Meredith and getting insight into both their psyches?*

She stood up and followed Bren out of the office after they were excused.

"When's the next flight?" he asked when they reached the privacy of her office. He sat down in her guest chair.

Being so close to him and remembering all the things that happened between them was bad enough, and now she'd be taking a trip with him. Alone!

Logging on to her computer, she found the airline's website and brought up the flight information. "There's a direct flight at seven thirty tomorrow morning." The sooner they got there and back, the better. Lounging around in airports gave them time to talk. She didn't want to give him time to talk about anything but the case.

"What time shall I pick you up?" he asked.

"I'll meet you there."

"It's no problem," he insisted.

"Thanks, but I'll be fine."

He crossed his arms over his chest, revealing the kind of shoulders Sanchez had tried to replicate. "You don't have to avoid me because you don't want to deal with what happened between us."

"You want to talk about it?" she shot back.

"I'm not against it, if that's what you mean."

Not against it? Geez. He sounded like a shrink. "This is neither the time nor the place," she said.

The intensity of his stare heated her cheeks. "You're right." He stood up and headed towards the door. "I'll see you tomorrow, Angel."

CHAPTER 9

Bren tried to make idle chitchat during the flight. Where did she work after college? When did she return to the island? Did she like her job? But she suspected, that like her, he still felt the strangeness of the abrupt end to their relationship in college, and their sudden re-association for a murder case.

After a few minutes, she pulled her attention away from him to review the list of questions she'd prepared to ask Meredith. Memories of her days with Meredith taunted her: from fun and loving mother at bedtimes to her crazy behavior before and after she killed someone.

Bren's glances burned a hole in the side of her face, but she refused to look at him and have to answer more of his obviously forced questions.

She was thankful he didn't ask her how she felt about seeing Meredith. She'd stopped calling her Mother the day Meredith was sentenced.

"Stop trying to analyze me, Bren."

"I never tried to an—"

Her stern look stopped him.

"Just trying to help," he offered.

"I don't need your help."

No one could help her. She'd learned that truth a long time ago.

The last time she'd seen Meredith, she was looking for answers to why she'd killed those men. She'd convinced herself all those years that Meredith had a valid reason. She was wrong.

She braced herself for what lay ahead when the airplane landed. There were too many memories: seeing Meredith, the taunting voices, and then leaving Bren. Each one was more heartbreaking than the other.

Angel unbuckled the seatbelt and reached for her bag as soon as the light went off. She and Bren made their way through the immigration lines quickly and were greeted with cool English breezes when they exited the airport. As they made their way to Broadmoor Hospital in a hired cab, she stated firmly, "I ask the questions, you make the observations."

He nodded and gave her a mock salute. "Aye, sir."

The cab pulled up to the building and she waited a moment for Bren to get out. She needed to prepare herself emotionally for the memories of the past on a collision course with her future.

The structure of the institute was massive: a building recognized for its architectural and historical significance. From certain angles, it looked like a brick house in the country, but from other angles, the tall stone walls and high fences told a different story.

Angel looked up to the top of the building. Somewhere inside was her mother, and possibly the key to solving her case. The last statement should've eased the stone cold sensation in her stomach, but it didn't.

The walk inside was a blur, the images and noises muffled and distanced as though she were watching someone else instead of experiencing it herself: from meeting the guard and being told the superintendent ward was in a meeting, to being taken inside the building where the inmates were housed.

Angel jumped at the sound of the metal gates banging closed behind her, shaking her out of her haze. Dread pressed against her like the weight of an elephant sitting slowly on her chest as every step took her closer to the woman she once called Mommy, and who had turned her childhood into a train wreck.

Beefy guards stood at each interlocking entrance, their eyes alert for any inmates who might try to make a run for it.

Inmates paced the halls, mumbling to themselves, shouting incoherently, or stared at the walls or ceilings with drug-induced, empty eyes.

"You okay?"

Every sweep of his eyes scorched her as they moved over her face.

She adjusted her jacket. Being around him now was worse than when they were in college. He still made her feel like a germ underneath a microscope one minute, and then he'd kiss her the next. "I'm fine," she lied, thankful her voice sounded more confident than she felt.

Her heart raced as she took a seat at the table and waited for Meredith to join them. Would Meredith recognize her or answer the questions?

The woman approaching them resembled Meredith, but was only a hollow shell who'd been reduced to a shallow face, thin frame, and eyes as empty as the other inmates'.

"Angel?" Meredith's face didn't register surprise or any other emotion. It was merely a question.

Angel nodded. *Was that it? All these years they hadn't seen each other and that was Meredith's response?*

Meredith looked at Bren. "Who he is?" Her voice was coarse, but her Caymanian accent was thick despite the years away from her home country.

Angel took a deep breath and convinced herself Meredith's lack of reaction was a good thing. Their relationship had died a long time ago and no situation would change that. "This is Bren MacDougal. We work together."

"Oh?" Meredith sat tentatively in the chair in front of them.

"How have you been?" Angel asked. She didn't want to make idle chatter with her mother, but she knew, like with any suspect, if she made her feel comfortable, she'd be more likely to open up and answer her questions or share information more easily.

Meredith eyed Bren uneasily before answering. "Alright. All tings considered."

"Are they treating you well?" Angel continued.

Meredith's glance bore into hers, as it had when she was a child and had done something wrong. "Well enough." She pulled her white jacket closer to her thin frame. "Wha you doing here, Angel? You didn't come all dis way to ask me des questions."

Angel let out the breath she was holding. "We need information."

"Wha information?" Meredith looked to Bren and then her.

"Has anyone visited you recently who wanted to know about the murders?" Angel was careful not to say *your murders.* Meredith appeared heavily medicated, but she didn't want to risk upsetting her.

"Why you wanna know?" Meredith pressed.

"Your hair was found at a recent crime scene."

She watched Meredith's face to see what emotions would erupt.

"So." Meredith shrugged.

"You haven't been in Cayman for twenty years," Angel said. She couldn't tell if her mother knew something or was merely avoiding the question. "And the murder was identical."

Meredith's facial wrinkles made waves as she contemplated and digested the words, before her eyes landed on Angel. "It's startin' again."

Angel's heart hitched in her throat. "What's starting again?"

"The curse," Meredith whispered, watching her for a reaction or confirmation of the truth. Angel kept her expression neutral, knowing Bren was observing.

"Curse?" Bren asked.

"It starts with the taunts until you wanna to pull ya hair out and then the sweet voices sayin' it okay and how good it'll feel."

Meredith gazed off in the distance as if reliving a lost or forgotten memory.

"How good what will feel?" Bren asked.

Angel glared at him in disapproval. The questions were for her to ask, not him. She planned to ask the questions on her list and nothing more.

"Killing. The blood splattering on your hands and the look in their eyes when they realize what you've done." Her voice heightened with excitement and a glint formed in her eyes before she pushed it back.

Angel hadn't expected her mother to answer with so much detail. Meredith had never spoken openly about the murders when she was a child. There hadn't been a need to.

"Do they still speak to you?"

"No. I think it's the medication."

Drugs had worked for her mother, so why not her?

"Who was your last visitor?" She shifted the conversation back to where it belonged, on the case. It didn't matter if there was a curse or if Meredith heard voices. In the end, her actions had sealed both their fates.

"Only one person since you. He said he was a reporter who wanted to interview me, but I knew he wasn't no reporter. He wanted to know tings about the killings no reporter would wanna know," Meredith said.

She avoided Meredith's pressing observation by making notes in her journal.

"You hearing dem, aren't you?" Meredith stretched across the table towards her.

Bren's gaze fell on her, as intense as Meredith's, as they waited for her to answer.

She pretended not to hear the question. "Can you describe him? Height, weight, if he had any distinguishing marks?"

"He wasn't tall. Light-skinned. Blond hair, but it didn't look real. He looked ordinary, no marks. He also asked a lotta questions 'bout you."

"Me?" She took a calming breath, and resisted the urge to look at Bren to see if he was studying her or Meredith.

"He wanted to know where you were living, and wha you were doin'. I told him I didn't know," she said with a shrug.

Angel scribbled in her notebook, but her mind filled with questions about the man her mother mentioned. *Why would he want to know about her? Was he the person committing the murders?*

"You gonna fight the voices, Angel? You were always a strong-willed child." Meredith ran a hand through her white-streaked hair. "Just like your father."

The space around Angel went silent. Meredith never told her who her father was.

The conversation was headed in a direction it didn't need to go, even if they were questions she wanted the answers to. It wasn't why they were here, and she certainly didn't want to discuss her family history with Bren sitting right there.

Meredith grabbed Angel's arm resting on the table. "I tried to save you by sending you ta church." She got a stern look from the guard, but she continued. "It was in vain; I see it in ya eyes. The harder you fight, the stronger de gonna get."

"I'm not going to ruin my life the way you did, Meredith," Angel responded calmly, but she wanted to shout that she'd never do that to people she loved.

"They only go away if you listen ta dem, but don't listen ta dem." Meredith reached out and grabbed Angel's other hand when she started to move it out of her reach. "Don't listen ta dem!" she yelled. Angel tried to pull her hands from her grasp, but Meredith's fingers dug deeper into her skin.

Her wild eyes bore into Angel as she screamed, "Don't listen ta dem!" again and again until Bren and two guards rushed forward. One pulled Meredith away and locked her hands behind her back, and the other injected a needle into her arm.

Bren's eyes were wide with a combination of fear and surprise. "You alright?" he asked when Meredith was out of the room.

She nodded, but didn't meet his gaze. She didn't want him to see the pain and hurt she was certain were in her eyes before she got them under control. "We should speak with the superintendent," she said, standing up.

He didn't answer, just watched her like a patient on a psychiatrist's couch who'd just revealed an unexpected dark secret.

They left the patient ward and headed to the superintendent, John Munson's, office. He was just as thick as the guards, but with a friendlier smile that reached his eyes. He apologized for not being able to meet them when they arrived, and motioned for them to take a seat.

"I heard your visit was a little scary." John's eyes searched Angel's face.

"It was expected," she said coolly, but John didn't appear convinced.

"Can you tell us about Meredith's visitors?" she asked.

"Other than yourself, there's been only one person." He pushed a piece of paper towards her. "A Gerard Smith."

It was an obvious alias, but she didn't allude to it. "What about letters?"

"There were a few, mostly from Christian groups or a victim's family. No marriage proposal, if that's what you mean," John joked.

"Can I have these?" she asked.

"Sure. They're copies."

She asked a couple more questions before she stood to leave. "Thank you for your time." She shook his extended hand before they left his office. She was thankful Bren was quiet the whole time, but she had a nagging feeling he was using it to watch her.

When the cab arrived moments after they got outside, the weight of the emotions that had pressed against her chest during her confrontation with Meredith didn't subside like she hoped.

***

Angel sat next to him in the cab stiff-backed, her expression as solemn as the day he'd first met her. He hadn't known what to expect when they went to interview Meredith, but he hadn't expected to hear about the curse again, or Meredith's violent reaction towards Angel at the end.

Even though Williams wanted him to study them, Bren wanted to know for himself. Being around Angel again had stirred up old feelings he'd tried hard to forget. When the opportunity to work in Cayman came up, he'd jumped at it, using it as an excuse to see her. He'd been too hurt when she left him to chase after her. When he found out about her mother, it stunned him, and he kept his distance until he could decide how to deal with it, but then weeks turned to months and it became easier to stay away than deal with it.

He reached across the seat to touch the hand that lay there, but she moved it away. Even now she didn't want comfort. Her strong will was something he admired about her, but unfortunately it was to the point she blocked out people even when she needed them. Was she afraid she'd hurt people the way her mother had?

He paid the cab driver when they reached the hotel and

followed Angel up the three flights of stairs to her room, which was right next door to his.

"Would ye like to talk?" he asked. "Ye shouldn't be alone after what happened today."

He placed his hand on her shoulder. She looked up at him and he remembered the times he'd made her laugh, and the moments they shared in chemistry class and in the library studying.

"How thoughtful to offer yourself, Bren." Her sarcasm sliced through him. "I suppose you want to have a nightcap and catch up on old times, too?"

He removed his hand from her shoulder. "It's me, Angel. I'm not some guy trying to get you into his room. We were friends once, remember?"

Her expression became cooler than he thought possible. "Friends?" She laughed cruelly. "Is that what we were?"

"I wanted to be more, ye know that." He knew today was difficult, but anger was the last emotion he expected.

Hazel eyes bore into him, studying his eyes and face.

"We could never be more," she replied, as though they were talking about the weather.

Her words and their indifference sliced his heart. *Don't torture yourself, Bren. There's no need to re-live your broken history together.*

"Goodnight, Angel."

"Goodnight, Bren."

She slipped inside her room and closed the door behind her.

He went into his own room and sat on the bed. Angel was driving him crazy. She was the most aggravating, stubborn woman he'd ever met. He slammed his hand against the bed but didn't get any satisfaction. What he really wanted to do in the hallway was to grab her shoulders and shake some sense into her. Couldn't she see what she was doing to herself? If he were honest, he'd say what she was doing to them, but the hard truth was there was no "them." Never had been and, according to her, never would be.

It shouldn't matter; it was better this way. But that didn't diminish the ache in the pit of his stomach or the urge to kiss her when she got near him. He ran his thumb and index finger along the top of his nose.

Forget it, Bren. Do what you came here to do. If you tangle yourself in Angel's life again, your heart is going to feel like it's going through a meat grinder.

He pushed himself off the bed and went to sit at the small desk in front of the queen-sized bed. He concentrated on what Meredith had said about the curse. A curse. It'd sounded like a bad joke, but he couldn't ignore the conviction in Meredith's voice or her words that Angel would give in to it eventually.

They called it a curse, but he suspected it was schizophrenia and nothing more. It was genetic, which might explain why Angel and other women in her family had experienced it. It even explained why Meredith might have killed those people.

As he and Angel worked together, things grew tenser. She froze when he came near her and put space between them before he could blink his eyes. She was worse than she'd been in college. What the hell had happened to her in the eight years since then?

He knew she'd worked in London, but had left that job to go back home. There was no indication from the other officers and CS Williams anything substantial had happened other than her wanting to change jobs.

He rubbed the tension from the back of his neck with his hand. A man who appeared obsessed with the murders and Angel had visited Meredith. It was a red flag, but was he really the killer? And if so, what was his reason? To get Angel's attention, or to frame her for murder? He wished he knew the answers.

How she'd managed to keep her reactions under control

even with her mother's outburst and her tight grip on Angel's arm amazed him. The marks of Meredith's fingers had remained on Angel's skin until they left the institute. It was only on the cab ride home, and when they had spoken in the hallway, that she showed any signs of emotion.

Angel was on the verge of an emotional breakdown and needed help. He was determined to do everything in his power to help her.

***

Angel leaned against the door and let the tears she'd been fighting since they left the institute fall freely. They wanted to come out in loud sobs, but she wouldn't let them.

{IYou won't be able to resist us. The words had resounded in her mind again and again in the cab ride back to the hotel, haunting her nearly as much as the taunting voices did. There were so many questions she had wanted to ask Meredith that had nothing to do with the case. The answer she wanted to know most was about her father. Who was he and did he know about her? Meredith had never wanted to discuss him when she asked why she didn't have a daddy. After Meredith was sentenced and sent to England, she convinced herself he didn't know about her and that was why he wasn't part of her life.

All those years, she'd thought Meredith was weak, giving in to the voices that told her to kill, but now she understood how keenly they'd tormented her. She intended to be stronger than her mother, but would she be able to keep it up for the rest of her life?

A mental hospital was the only place for her, but she shivered at the thought of spending the rest of her life in a drug-induced haze, with her behavior and actions analyzed every day.

She dialed the number for the front desk and asked for

the location of the nearest liquor store. She couldn't charge the alcohol to the room, and even if she paid it back, she didn't want anyone knowing she'd cleaned out the minibar. It would raise more than a few eyebrows.

The voices hadn't troubled her since she'd landed at Heathrow, but she wouldn't take the chance they'd leave her alone tonight.

She poured two full glasses of vodka down her throat five minutes after she'd returned to her room. She sat on the small loveseat and turned on the news. An empty bottle remained three hours later, before she turned off the TV and staggered to the bed. The voices were silenced, but when she closed her eyes to go to sleep, blood and mayhem were her bedmates.

CHAPTER 10

Angel sat in Williams' office while he read the report she'd prepared. She'd neglected to mention what Meredith had said about the curse and the final words she screamed, and not because it would make her appear a suspect. She was already a suspect. Her connection to Meredith, and that Meredith's hair had been found at the scene of the crime, made Angel at the very least a person of interest.

This was etched on the face of Williams on the occasion he looked up at her in the MIR, and on the officers every morning when she passed them on her way to her office. Some looked at her accusingly while others avoided her more than usual.

Next to her, Bren remained silent.

"Can you excuse us a moment, Professor MacDougal?" Williams asked.

Bren nodded and left the room.

Not good.

"Is this everything?" Williams attempted to strip away her confidence with his stern gaze.

"Everything pertaining to the case."

Did Bren already speak with him about what happened and wanted to know why she had left it out of the report? Was it really relevant to the case? She didn't think so.

"What else happened?"

The forceful stare made her feel like a suspect whose

secret was about to be found out.

She eyed him warily. He was another memory from her childhood she didn't want; she knew she couldn't trust him. He was part of the attempted international public cover-up of Meredith's murders, and Angel being there was a blatant reminder. The MLAs at the time didn't want the story to become public, fearful it would hurt tourism. Who'd want to visit an island where the guests were being slaughtered by a local serial killer?

Angel shrugged. "She lost her temper when she didn't get the reaction she wanted from me."

An eyebrow rose, suggesting curiosity. "What reaction was she expecting?"

"An emotional one," she said coolly.

The leather chair groaned when he shifted.

It was no secret she was known as the Ice Princess around the station. Her emotions were never out of control.

"What triggered it?" Williams asked.

Should she give him that kind of ammunition, or let him get it from Bren?

"It was personal."

He didn't respond, merely watched her with his ageless brown eyes while silence and discomfort filled his office.

"I shouldn't be on this case," she blurted. She knew it; so did the other officers. Why did he continue to insist she stay on? Was he hoping she'd fail or slip and give herself up as the killer?

"Under normal circumstances I would agree with you, but these aren't normal circumstances. Your connection to the murders, although unfortunate, is useful. Besides, I've got clearance from the police commissioner, if you're concerned about the legality," he said confidently.

"I was only ten when Meredith was taken away. I barely remember what happened, and try to block out the bits I do remember." She lied. She wished she could forget, but the voices and old memories that disturbed her dreams wouldn't let her.

"You didn't see your mother dumping bodies in the neighborhood outhouse?" He leaned forward, his elbows resting against the edge of his desk.

"Would you want to remember that or that your mother killed five innocent people?" she asked, shifting her hands to clasp them in her lap. He hadn't questioned her, but even now she could hear the prompting in the constables' voices, trying to get her to admit seeing Meredith so they could use it against her.

Silence hung in the air of his small office. "You're staying on this case."

"Yes, sir." She stood up to leave.

"Look, Angel, I don't like this situation either, but it isn't about us. It's about finding the killer and stopping more innocent people from dying."

"Agreed."

It was also about him leaving unsolved murder cases just as he was about to retire. She didn't know if his determination was real, or if he was just worried about his reputation.

"Send in MacDougal."

She nodded and left.

The walk back to her office had her mind racing with questions Williams would ask Bren. *How much would he say?* She found Bren in her office. "The CS wants to see you."

Bren studied her with his aqua eyes that saw places of herself she didn't want him or anyone to see and know. She hated that about him.

She avoided his scrutiny, despite wanting to blurt out to keep quiet about what Meredith said, and watched his back as he left. She didn't like the CS knowing and had no intention of Sanchez, Johnson, or Ebanks getting wind of it. Until she officially became a suspect, she planned to do everything she could to prevent anyone from hearing about a curse.

If she wasn't living through it, it'd be one big joke, but there was nothing to laugh about.

College was supposed to be a fresh start for her, a chance to get away and be free from the stigma of Meredith and her family history. In England, Meredith was just another crazy person who couldn't be connected to her. Nobody would know who she was and she'd planned to enjoy every minute of it. The joke had been on her. Trying to open up and have fun was like being a wayward teenager who was forced to stay home and study to improve their grades. It was worse when she'd met Bren and got a glimpse at a chance at happiness and a life. She'd been horribly wrong. She had no intention of making the same mistake again.

CHAPTER 11

She was perfect. Beautiful, with a worldly appearance. He knew it despite not exchanging words with her. Elegant clothing hugged her frame, lean from exercise. A confident smile kissed her lips. But, more importantly, her dark hair and wide eyes reminded him of Angel.

"You here alone?"

Sparkling gray eyes looked up at him. "Why, yes I am. Care to join me?"

Eager. He liked that. It meant getting to the part he liked faster. He nodded and took a seat next to her in the booth.

He knew it was risky returning to the same place, but he had to. This is where Meredith had killed her second victim and it had to be the same. Angel would want it that way. He needed it that way.

"Where you from?" he asked, snaking his arm around her shoulder, sensing she wouldn't care from the way her eyes had checked him out before he sat down. She was here for one reason.

"North Carolina. I'm Charlotte. What about you?" she asked, seductively licking the moisture of her drink from her bottom lip.

He wanted to laugh at the name she'd given him. Definitely fake. Charlotte, from North Carolina. *Who did she think she was fooling?*

"Does it matter?" His hand moved to caress her neck and he watched anticipation flicker in her eyes.

Exhilaration fluttered in his stomach that soon he'd have her pressed against the mattress, her eyes growing vacant while his knife slid across her throat. He observed the crowd of the kids on the dance floor, their bodies moving in time with the music beneath the changing lights that cascaded shadows against their scantily clad bodies and the floor of the club.

Angel was the one he wanted seated next to him, and if he had a choice it wouldn't be in this seedy place, but somewhere nice. Maybe the Ritz, where she'd be treated properly with delicious food, flattering lighting, and soft music. He'd have her in his arms, dancing and laughing. He'd never heard her laugh before, but he knew she would with him. Her laughter would be his alone.

"Are you okay?"

The touch of a hand on his shoulder pulled him back to the club and he turned and gave her the smile he liked to call "melt their panties." He saved his real smiles for Angel. "Sure." He leaned closer to Charlotte. "Wanna get out of here?" he whispered seductively in her ear, his fingertips caressing her bare shoulders.

"Alright."

As they staggered down the dreary hallway, he imagined it was the lavish hallway of the Ritz, and it was Angel's hand he held as they made their way to a room filled with champagne and flowers and not smelly carpet and questionable bedding.

Soon.

He walked in behind Charlotte when she opened her room door. She'd gotten one of the nicer rooms, but it still reeked of "cheap," smoke, and other things that made his nose want to reject them.

"Why don't you slip into something comfortable while I

get us drinks?" he suggested. He kissed, and then nibbled her shoulder.

Charlotte smiled seductively and headed to the bathroom.

All too easy.

He opened the bottle of red wine and poured two glasses. He dropped Rohypnol into her glass and set it on the edge of the counter.

Moments later, she came out of the bathroom in just her lace underwear, her makeup refreshed. She picked up the glass of wine and took a drink.

He turned on the radio of the clock sitting on the nightstand. He scrolled through the stations until he found the right music.

"Dance for me," he ordered softly.

Charlotte swayed her body seductively in time to the music, but as the song ended she started stumbling and fell back on the bed.

She laughed and spread herself for his viewing enjoyment. "This wine is going straight to my head."

Not to mention what she had at the club, and what he'd drugged her with. He strolled over to the bed, sat on the edge, and caressed her face and then ran his hands along her neck. She moaned and arched her body towards his hand as it roamed over her skin before returning to her face. His fingers gently ran along her lips.

He watched her eyes grow dim as she attempted to keep them open. Soon the drugs would fully kick in and he'd get to work. It would be easy to squeeze the life out of her, but he needed her murder to be the same as Meredith's murders.

"Sshh," he whispered when Charlotte's eyes grew wide with fear as the reality of what she'd gotten herself into sunk in. He pressed his hand over her mouth, smearing her lipstick. The moisture and spit of her mouth pressed into his palm, along with the vibrations of her light, silenced screams.

"I know this wasn't what you were expecting, but you're

not her and your death is for her."

Her screams vibrated against his hand again, this time weaker. Annoyance and excitement tickled him. "Are you going to make this difficult? I hope so."

She stilled and he chuckled. Right now she was probably thinking there was a chance he'd have mercy, end it quickly, but she'd be wrong. Killing her was a means to an end, but that didn't mean he couldn't enjoy it.

Charlotte's body stilled beneath him. He removed his hands and took the knife from his sports jacket. He ran his fingertips down her long neck just before he slashed it. As the blood dripped onto her chest, staining the pale skin, he saw Angel's face and heard the thrill in her voice as she agreed to marry him.

Soon. Soon, they'd be together forever.

CHAPTER 12

Angel's hand shook as she reached for the doorknob. Only two weeks had passed since the first body was found. *So much for having a month between murders.* The suspect had a shorter down time, which was bad news for everyone.

She closed her eyes and took a quick breath before entering the room.

The body sat upright, leaned against the headboard. The victim's eyes were open—her expression vacant but accusing.

Excitement shot through Angel at the site of her slashed throat.

{IYes. Yes.

The voices whispered sweetly, tempting her with the thrill of the kill.

It was a lie. There was never any sign of happiness in Meredith's eyes the next day. It was a look of torment she hoped to never experience.

"Please stay in the doorway until everything is processed. I don't want to risk anything of your DNA being left behind," she said to Bren. "I'll leave the door open so you can observe what you need to."

He nodded briefly. His skin tone had dulled and his mouth quivered. He was ready to heave whatever he'd eaten for breakfast that morning. Seeing and smelling the body and being in the midst of a crime scene was nothing like studying the photos. He'd now just learned this the hard way.

"It's different in person, isn't it?" she asked.

Bren nodded and gazed about the room quickly.

"Get some fresh air. I'll be here awhile," Angel told him. He rushed away.

The wounds on this victim were the same as those of the first murder. This body was positioned differently than the first, but still in the same position as the second victim from twenty years ago.

She finished processing the room for evidence just as Bren returned.

"Exactly the same body placement and it's the same room as Meredith's second murder," Bren said as he came to stand beside her.

"That should also narrow down the suspects," she said. She didn't meet his gaze, but looked about the room to make sure she hadn't missed anything.

"What do ye mean?" he asked.

"Not many people had access to the photos of the victims, which could mean it's someone who has or had access to the information," she replied.

"True, but how secure is the information? If everything is electronic, they could've hacked the computer system and obtained the information that way too," he said.

"Well, that's one downside to technology. I just scanned all the photos for that case last year. If I hadn't, the chances of the killer getting his hands on the information would've been more difficult." She looked around the room again.

"Maybe, or maybe they would've found a more inventive way to get the information they wanted." He put his nose in the crook of his arm. "Are we good here? Can we leave now?"

The body wasn't even dead twenty-four hours. If he thought it stunk now, he wouldn't make it five minutes in the morgue with Jackson. "You can wait for me outside. Once the EMT picks up the body, we can leave."

"I'll wait with you," he replied, but his eyes said he

wanted to get the hell out.

"I'll be fine. You're not used to being around dead bodies. You should go." She pointed outside.

"You're used to dead bodies?" he asked a little too quickly.

"Yes. I worked in London for six years. I saw and smelled a lot of dead bodies." Her eyes held his sternly.

"I didn't mean to imply anything." His expression was apologetic.

She closed the lid on her evidence bag. "Sure you didn't."

He watched her with those penetrating eyes before he left.

"Ready for pickup?" Jackson asked from the doorway.

"What are you doing here, Jackson?" Angel asked. He never came to collect bodies. It was usually done by the EMTs.

He shrugged. "I wanted to see the site where the body was found," he said cryptically. "The EMTs are on their way, but I thought I'd check things out first."

She was about to say it was the same as where the first was found, but realized Jackson hadn't seen the first site, merely heard about it. He had helped with identifying the weapon from the last case, but she hoped that didn't mean he suddenly considered himself a constable.

"I heard you and Professor MacDougal went to college together," he said casually.

"Yes, we were lab partners," she replied.

How had the conversation suddenly turned personal?

"So, not some guy you dated?"

His tone was casual, but she studied him with a sideways glance. He never asked her personal questions. Jackson was a character she had yet to figure out. *Was he painfully shy or did he just like dead bodies better than living people?*

"We never dated."

Being friends for four years and sleeping together once wasn't dating, although it was as close to dating as she'd ever gotten.

Jackson seemed satisfied by her answer and returned to asking questions about the scene from the doorway.

Moments later, the EMT arrived and placed the body in the bag. She and Jackson followed behind them. They passed Bren talking with Johnson and Ebanks.

"He's friendly," Jackson observed.

"He is."

It hadn't taken Bren long to get the other constables to warm up to him. A case of Blue Mountain Coffee and beef patties was all it took.

"I bet he was popular at school." The wistfulness in Jackson's voice hinted he may have wanted to have been the same. That surprised her. He didn't seem the type to care about things like that.

"He was."

One of the most popular at school, but she didn't tell Jackson, thinking it might make him feel worse. She wasn't liked at the force for obvious reasons, but he stuck out like a sore thumb and probably did in school too.

"We haven't had this much excitement since…" Jackson started.

"Since the last murder?" she answered for him.

Excitement? Was that how he saw it?

He flashed her a crooked tooth grin. "I was going to say never, but you're right."

What was it about the murders that thrilled him so much? Was it having dead bodies to examine?

"People are dead, Jackson—innocent people who didn't deserve to die. That's not something to celebrate." She regretted the harshness of her tone the moment she saw hurt flicker in his eyes.

"I'm sorry," he said sheepishly.

"Me too." It wasn't Jackson's fault he liked dissecting dead bodies. It's what made him good at his job. "See you at the hospital."

Jackson nodded and got into his car.

After the fiasco with the press and crowd of people from the first murder, the police perimeter was set farther back from the hotel to keep people and the camera crews at a distance.

She went to her car, where Bren was waiting.

"Got everything?" he asked. He was leaning casually against the edge, oblivious of the crowd of people and the press yelling to get his attention.

She nodded. He was analyzing her. She could see it in the narrowing of his eyes and the straight line of his mouth. She didn't like it, but there was nothing she could do about it.

"Have dinner with me tonight," he stated casually.

"Why?"

Damn, she should've just said no instead of leaving the door open. She was surprised he had waited this long to ask. She knew he'd been chomping at the bit to talk to her the moment the plane touched down in Cayman from London.

"To eat?" he said sarcastically.

She gave him another sideways glance.

"Okay, to talk," he admitted.

As they drove away, she looked out the window at the passing scenery. Things had been strained between them since they returned from England. They weren't uncivil, but the tension was so thick that Johnson had mentioned it. She'd told him to mind his own business.

"I don't think that's a good idea," she said finally.

He let out an exasperated sigh. "Look, Angel. Things have been hard for ye with this case and that visit with yer mother, but I'm not the enemy."

His eyes were on the road so he couldn't see her watching him. He was right. If she could talk to anyone

73

without worry about them sharing it with someone, it was Bren. But that's not what bothered her. She didn't like he thought of her as research because of her past history or that he found her behavior fascinating.

Pain clutched her chest. She needed to talk to someone and maybe talking would ease the tension between them. Who knew how long they'd be working together.

"Let's make it at your place. I don't want anyone to see us socializing in public," she said candidly.

"Agreed." He put on the indicator to take them downtown.

"Should I bring anything?"

"Just yourself and a bottle of wine."

Was he remembering that she'd been drunk on wine the night they kissed? "I don't drink," she responded quickly.

Bren gave her a crooked grin. Her stomach flip-flopped and made her remember their only night together. The heat of his breath in her ears and the sweet, naughty words he whispered as he moved inside her.

Maybe dinner wasn't such a good idea after all.

CHAPTER 13

Angel knocked on Bren's apartment door later that evening and tugged at her blouse. She was dressed more casually than when she had been at the office, now wearing a silk blouse and Capri pants. She wanted to keep as much skin covered as possible. Damn but she hated the way he unnerved her and made her doubt the confidence she normally clung to with ease.

The door opened shortly after the first knock.

He checked his watch. "Right on time."

"For you." She handed him the bottle of wine when she got inside. His apartment smelled like him, warm and inviting, but with a hint of masculine appeal that tugged at the senses. It was certainly tugging at hers.

"Would you like a glass?"

"No, thanks." She circled his living room, merely checking things out, but then she realized she was looking for photos of women in his past.

It was nicely decorated, and not the typical bachelor pad with sparse or bulky furniture and the photo on the wall that made you think, "What the hell is it?" If she knew Bren, he'd brought in a design company to decorate.

On a table behind his couch was a photo with his parents at his college graduation, and next to it was the one his roommate had taken of Bren with his arms around her. She glanced around the room quickly to see if there were any other pictures with him and other women, but there were none.

Why had he kept it? The question itched at her mind and she wanted to scratch that itch and ask him, but knew she couldn't. It would lead to talking about their friendship, their one night together, and her disappearance the next morning—not only from his bed, but his life.

"I ordered Chinese. It should be here in a few minutes." He uncorked the bottle of red wine. "Ye still like fried wontons and beef broccoli, right?"

She nodded. *He remembered.* She let her thoughts entertain the possibility he still cared about her, before she shoved them aside. Of course he remembered. She was a creature of habit and they ate Chinese every Friday night while they studied.

"So, what happens after we eat?" Her tone was stern, but she realized too late that she had, in a small way, implied something naughty. *Not good.*

"What do ye want to happen after we eat?" It was asked as if she was sitting on his couch for a one-hour session.

She smirked.

"I think it's important for us to talk about what happened at the institute, with your mother." He moved to sit on the couch and patted the seat next to him for her to join him.

She went to sit at the single chair across from the couch. "Why?" she asked, although she knew the direction his thoughts were heading.

"The killer is obviously fascinated with you and your mother. He might be trying to implicate you as a suspect," he said carefully.

"People already think I killed those women, Bren," she countered. "I told CS Williams I shouldn't be on the case, but he insisted, so there's little I can do."

"I didn't know that." His face looked perplexed.

"You can see it on their faces when they look at me. Even before the murders started, they thought I was like

Meredith." Her voice was edged with suppressed pain straining to get out.

"I thought it was because they called you 'Ice Princess.'" He gave her one of his heart-stopping grins she was certain had melted the knees of several women, herself included.

She laughed. Something she hadn't done in a very long time. His ability to make her laugh was what had attracted her in college.

"Isn't that better?"

She nodded and relaxed the stiff arch of her back against the soft leather chair, thankful he decided to change the subject, at least for the moment.

Five minutes later, the food arrived and they sat in silence, neither wanting to break the peacefulness between them.

"What did your mother's rant mean?"

His question came out of nowhere and she threw up her wall of defense. "Just the ravings of someone who's spent too much time imprisoned and medicated."

"True, but that's not entirely the case, is it? I got a copy of your mother's therapy files while we were in England and although there's no mention of it in the police reports here, she confessed to blackouts leading up to the murders."

Her heart stopped and her hand stilled on its way to her water bottle before she put it in motion again. *Did he notice?*

She shrugged. "A lot of psychopaths have blackouts."

"Do you?"

"Are you worried I'm the murderer and I'm going to get rid of you?" She tried to make her voice sound sarcastic and light, but failed.

"That would be careless, wouldn't it?" he said with a grin.

"I used to be a scene of crime officer, so I'd have an advantage."

His eyes studied her intently. "You're not a murderer."

77

"How do you know that?" she asked, and relaxed in the chair.

"I just do," he insisted.

"Really? It doesn't bother you my mother is a serial killer?" She held her breath, despite her casual tone.

"No," he said without hesitation.

"I don't believe you. You don't want a murderer in your life any more than anyone would."

"Your mother was the murderer, not you." His tone was soft and low.

"Her blood is my blood."

"I don't believe that!" He reached out to take her hand, but she shifted her arm and body out of his grasp.

"Really? Then why didn't you contact me when you first got here? You've been on the island for over a year, Bren!" Her tone was an iced lake.

Shut the hell up, Angel. It doesn't matter why he didn't reach out.

His eyes met hers and an apology flickered in them, but the words didn't make it to his lips.

"Goodbye Bren." She stood up and headed to the front door.

"You left without a word the day after you made love to me," he blurted.

She stopped, but didn't turn around.

"After you told me you loved me," he added. His accent thickened with each statement he'd made.

She stood there with her back turned to him for several seconds before leaving. He didn't try to stop her, and she was glad. There was nothing he could say to make her believe he didn't think she was like her mother—nothing!

CHAPTER 14

Angel's stiff posture and cold demeanor met Bren when he got to her office the next morning.

"Coffee?" He handed her a large caramel macchiato.

She took the coffee from his hand, but didn't look at him.

He hadn't gotten any sleep the night before, after she left. His emotions were still raw from their argument and memories he wanted to forget. His dinner invite was to get her to open up and talk about what had happened with her mother, for her to tell him what was going on in that pretty head of hers, but it had backfired. This wasn't a good time to talk about where they had left off. A killer was on the loose and catching him or her was more important than their past.

They had met with CS Williams early that morning and he wanted them to speak with people from Meredith's family for anyone acting out of character recently.

"Who do ye suggest that can be discreet?" He took a sip of his coffee and met her with the expression he generally used with his students when he posed questions in class.

She leaned back in her chair. "My Aunt Maisy," she said quietly. "She raised me."

Had her family members ostracized her the way some members of the force had? He longed to reach out to her and tell her how sorry he was for her unhappy childhood and that she'd misunderstood his words last night, but he decided against it.

79

"Sanchez is looking into 'Gerard Smiths' traveling to the island over the past five to ten years. It's not much of a lead, but it's a start. He's also looking into the dates of any men traveling from England to Cayman around the time Gerard visited Meredith at the institute."

She made notes in her notepad.

"This killer is dangerous, Angel." He didn't want to scare her, but he wanted her to understand what kind of person she was up against.

"I know that."

It was then that he realized she wasn't afraid that someone had pulled her into the dangerous game he was playing, duplicating her mother's murders. She was good at hiding her emotions, but this was different.

She hadn't answered him when he asked her about blackouts. He honestly believed the Angel he knew wouldn't kill anyone, but did he really know her that well? Was there something in her past darker than her mother's history? He'd hoped seeing her with Meredith would give him a glimpse into her psyche that might answer the questions that Williams was looking for, but he was burdened with more questions. Perhaps he'd get his chance today with her aunt.

"Are you ready to go?" Angel asked.

"Aye."

He grabbed the cup of coffee he'd set down on her desk earlier.

The heat of the sun warmed his face, and the humidity in the air stole his breath when they stepped outside the station and headed to Angel's car.

Silence hovered between them as they drove through downtown to where she had grown up. A mixture of houses lined the street she turned down off the main road. There were old wooden ones, new concrete ones, and the remaining were under construction or a combination of concrete and wood.

They pulled up in front of a pink wooden house that was

decades older than the ones around it. They got out of the car and walked up the short distance to the house. Wind blew the dirt yard into their faces and onto the colorful, flowerless plants close to the house.

Angel knocked tentatively at the front door.

A black wrinkled face peered from behind the wooden door. "I was wondering when you'd come see me." Dark eyes assessed him from head to toe before they settled back on Angel. "Come in, child," she greeted Angel, opening the door wider.

Bren wiped his feet on the welcome mat before following Angel inside.

The woman motioned them towards the plastic-covered couch and then went about closing the blinds and windows. "Nosy neighbors," she said with disgust. "Who dat is?" She pointed her chin at him.

"Bren MacDougal. He's helping with the…case." Angel chose her words carefully. "Bren, this is my Aunt Maisy."

They gave each other a friendly smile.

"Nice to meet you."

He extended his hand, but she merely looked at it, as if it were a foreign object.

"Can he be trusted?" her aunt asked pointedly, not caring that he could hear her.

"It depends on what you talk about," Angel said, and shifted in her seat. "He's a consultant CS Williams asked to help with the case."

A whimsy smirk curled Maisy's lips. "I bet he is." Her plump frame glided about the room before sitting on the single chair across from the couch. "So, wha you all want?" she asked, although her gaze was on him.

Straight to the point, just like Angel, Bren thought with a grin.

"We went to visit Meredith," Angel said, looking down at her hands on her lap.

"You went to see that witch after what happened last time?" Maisy shook her head in disbelief.

The venom in her voice surprised Bren, but he guessed it was because she had raised Angel and was protective of her.

Maisy straightened her posture. "Wha she said?"

Angel looked at him briefly before answering. "She told me about the curse."

She didn't mention the voices, but maybe it was because Maisy already knew, Bren reasoned.

"I kept a lot of tings from you as a child, but not that blasted curse of the women in dis family," Maisy responded.

Angel adjusted the collar of her blouse. "Meredith said the same thing."

"Did she say anything else?" Maisy asked.

"No."

"What is the curse?" Bren asked.

Both women looked at him and then each other as though they were deciding who'd be the one to tell him.

Maisy stood up and moved towards the window. She peeked outside, as if to make sure no one was out there listening.

"The story been around so long, nobody really know for sure wha true and wha hearsay."

He waited patiently for her to continue while she paced before him, but no answer came.

"But you're fine," Angel argued.

"They say it only affect certain family members," Maisy answered.

"Like Meredith?" Angel asked.

"Do you mean to tell me other women in this family have murdered people?" Bren couldn't believe what he was hearing.

Maisy turned to look at him as if remembering he was there. "No. They didn't murder anybody, but killed themselves or went crazy. Ain't no crazy hospital here."

"But why? I don't understand." Angel's voice was heavy.

"I know you don't, child. They say a woman from our family played around with Obeah so she could talk to her dead husband, and sold her family's souls to do it." Maisy put her hand on Angel's shoulder.

Obeah. The word was foreign to his vocabulary before coming to the Caribbean. If he'd heard this story without knowing Angel or her mother, or witnessed the conviction both of them expressed in their belief, he would have laughed at the very idea of it. But it didn't matter what he thought; it was real to them.

"Why didn't you tell me this before?" Angel asked.

"You was too young, child, and ya didn't show no signs so I thought ever'ting was alright," she defended.

"Everything isn't okay," Angel stammered, before she composed herself. "Has it ever affected any men?"

"Not that I know of."

As he watched Angel's interaction with her aunt, he'd expected more warmth, a hug, but nothing. What a lonely life she must've had after her mother was convicted. "What about someone from her father's side of the family?" Bren asked.

Maisy's eyes snapped to Angel. "She told you who your father was?"

"No," Angel said, so sadly it tore at his heart. He couldn't imagine something so important being kept from her. *Was it because her father had his own dark secrets?*

"Can you tell us what happened to the other women?" Bren asked. Angel had said everything wasn't okay. He wanted to know what she meant, but he couldn't ask her now.

"You hard a hearin' or wha? They kill themselves or went crazy," Maisy replied.

Someone was getting defensive.

"What was their behavior before it started? Did something trigger it?" he asked.

83

Maisy was pensive before answering. "Meredith said she heard voices telling her to do bad tings and she had terrible nightmares."

"Are there any other women in your family right now who might be affected?" Angel's face was strained and he wished he could put his arm around her. Maybe Maisy had heard something from other family members about strange behaviors that might lead them to the killer.

Maisy shook her head. "All da children from the past two generations except Angel have been boys. I tink it's God's way of cleansing our family."

"Is it possible it could have passed onto the women in her father's family?" Angel didn't know who her father was, but he suspected from Maisy's earlier reaction that she knew, although he couldn't imagine why she would keep it from Angel.

Maisy shook her head. "He don't have any udder children."

Bren watched as Angel's gaze turned towards her aunt. He thought her tan face would turn red.

"You know who he is and you didn't tell me? Who is it?!" Angel sat on the edge of the couch as if she'd attack if Maisy didn't give her the answer she wanted.

Sadness filled Maisy's eyes. "You na ready to know who he is, child. It would only bring you pain."

"I'm already in pain, Aunt Maisy!" Angel shot off the couch. "How could you do this to me? All these years you knew and never told me?"

The muscles in Angel's jaw worked overtime as she contained her emotions and sat back down. "Does he know? Will he tell me if I asked?"

"No, he don know either. Meredith lied to him."

Bren could feel the frustration pouring out of her. He couldn't blame her. He was becoming agitated himself.

"Meredith is never going to tell me. You don't think I

can handle it. He doesn't know. Is anyone ever going to tell me or am I going to go to my grave without knowing my father?" Angel bellowed.

Maisy lowered her eyes. "Yo'll find out when the time is right," she said quietly.

Angel stood up. "When the time is right? Like when I'm wandering the streets talking to myself, or after I've murdered someone!" Her voice grew louder with every word.

Bren had never seen her so angry before, ever. Her reaction was warranted given the situation, but it still surprised him that she'd reacted in front of him.

Maisy didn't answer.

Angel's hands clenched at her sides before she stormed off. The stomping of her weight made the boards of the floor creak louder than when they had arrived. She turned halfway to the door. "I won't be coming back here. Ever."

She glared at Maisy as if she planned to go back in and strangle the answer out of her. He could tell from Angel's strained expression that she wanted to say more, but didn't.

Bren stood up to leave and catch up with Angel, who was almost to the door.

Maisy's voice stopped them both. "If ever'ting isn't alright, Angel, you needa know…the curse started on Meredith's thirtieth birthday."

By started, he knew Maisy meant it was the first time Meredith killed someone.

It was four weeks before Angel's thirtieth birthday.

CHAPTER 15

{IYou know you want to do it. Kill.

The voice echoed softly, seductively. Angel took another large gulp of vodka.

{IIImagine. The feel of the blood on your fingertips.

She took another and then another, until the bottle was gone and so were the voices. The news blaring from the TV in the distance lulled her to sleep.

The phone ringing shook Angel from her fog of alcohol-induced sleep. She reached for the phone and tried without success to hide the slur in her voice.

"Angel, it's me. Are you alright?"

Damn it! Bren.

"Yes," she groaned when her head pulsed.

"Why aren't you answering the door? I've been outside your flat for ten minutes."

She could hear the worry in his voice.

"Go away. This is not a good time."

Not now. She couldn't let him see her like this.

"It's never a good time for a murder, but we need tae be there."

DAMN!

"Give me a minute," she said. She hung up the phone and peeled herself off the couch before stumbling to the bathroom. After a quick hot shower and a couple of pain killers, she headed to the front door.

When she reached the door, she saw, to her horror, that all the locks were unbolted. Her nightly ritual of bolting them all to keep her in and away from the things the voices chanted for her to do went out the window. *Had she locked them before she started drinking?* God help her, she couldn't remember.

Meredith had mentioned blackouts, but she didn't have any. *Did she?* She suddenly remembered those mornings when she'd felt physically tired even though she'd gone to bed early. *Was something happening while she slept?*

The slash of a knife across someone's neck. Blood splattering on her hands and clothing. Screaming and horrible laughter. They were her dreams lately. Were they something worse than nightmares? Were they suppressed memories from the killings? The victims' faces were a blur so she couldn't see them clearly, not even to tell if they were male or female.

She hadn't been drinking the night the second murder occurred, but did that really mean something didn't happen after she went to bed? Was it too early to clear herself as a suspect?

Her stomach lurched at the thought she'd killed someone and to her horror it wasn't from distaste but excitement. *It was getting worse.*

Her hand shook as she opened the door to let Bren in.

She cringed inwardly under his scrutinizing gaze. It was as though he could see past her façade of a hot shower, clean clothes, and toothpaste to the truth of what she looked like moments earlier.

"I thought ye didn't drink?" He glanced behind her.

Turning around, she saw what he had: an empty vodka bottle on the coffee table.

Heat rushed to her cheeks. Avoiding his gaze, she mumbled, "Only once in a while."

Bren remained silent as his eyes grazed over her apartment, making her wish she'd cleaned up before opening the door. Chinese takeout boxes from last night littered the coffee table, keeping the vodka bottle company, along with discarded articles of clothing splashed across the couch.

"I just need to get my purse."

Angel rushed to her bedroom, grabbed her bag, and rushed back to where he stood. "Let's go."

His eyes bore through her, their depths filled with unasked questions and an analysis that said he saw her pain.

She held her breath as his brows knotted in contemplation. *Not now, Bren.*

"Yeah."

There would never be a good time for the questions she suspected he wanted to ask.

"I'll drive," he said.

Angel didn't argue, but followed him downstairs, away from her apartment, and to his car.

***

Silence kept them company on the drive to the crime scene. Bren was still in shock at the sound of Angel's voice on the phone and the sight of her when she opened the door. The slur in her voice said she'd been drinking and even having showered and done her hair, the redness and shadows under her eyes couldn't be hidden. Neither could the fear that speckled her eyes. What would she have looked like if she'd opened the door before getting ready?

Except for the mess in the living room, her flat had been meticulously clean and organized, like Angel. She had lied about her drinking. *Was it yet another secret she kept? What else was she lying to him about or keeping from him?* Guilt stung him at his own secret that he was also there to evaluate her.

The number of locks on the inside of the door shocked

him. Why would someone need that many bolts on their door on an island as small and generally safe as Cayman? They didn't look new, so it wasn't to protect herself from the killer. *So what or who was she trying to keep out?*

"Where are we headed?" Angel asked.

"Boilers?" That was the name CS Williams had given him, but he had to ask for directions.

"Are you sure?" Angel looked at him with wide-eyed terror.

"Yes, why?" *What was up with her today?*

"No reason."

He didn't miss the tremble of her voice or the tightening of her hands on the handbag sitting on her lap.

"Well, the killer has been mimicking her killings. It's probably just another way he's following the pattern. That information was in the report, right?" he assured her.

She nodded stiffly.

Was it her aunt's secrets that unsettled her or was it because of her fast-approaching thirtieth birthday? He wished to hell she would talk to him.

When he pulled off the main road, police cars and constables blocked the narrow street. Onlookers lined the police barricades, trying to get a glimpse of the scene. Mixed in the crowd were Daniel from the Cayman Newsroom and his camera crew.

Angel's tension filled the small space of the car so that she pulled the cap on her head further down her face, making him wonder if it was to hide from him or from the crowd they drove through.

After parking the car, he followed her to the scene and braced himself not only mentally, but physically, for what would be awaiting them in the small wooden structure.

"This is the third murder, Angel. When are you going to turn yourself in?" Daniel shouted as he motioned for the cameraman to follow her.

The noise of talking people went deadly silent and everyone's gaze, including the constables', turned to Angel, who had stopped in mid step. She didn't turn around but kept walking.

"It's time to stop the murders, Angel, and get help!"

Daniel and his crew had managed to push past the constables trying to hold back the crowds.

Angel kept walking, but her back was straighter and her jaw clenched.

"That's Inspector Mason to you, Daniel! Now get back behind the line and let the constables do their job," Sanchez barked.

Daniel scowled at him, but did what he was told when Sanchez signaled two constables to help him.

The remaining constables dispersed against the rusting metal fencing as Angel made her way to the scene. Behind the fence, large tree branches stretched across the metal like snarled wooded arms, shading out the sunlight. Fallen almond seeds lay scattered on the ground. Long shadows cascaded along the narrow gravel path and accentuated each constable she passed.

Wooden houses, dark and dingy, were staggered on the pathway, their outside frames peeling like burnt flesh. A whirlwind of air whipped up the dirt and sand in the front yards and curtains opened to reveal rounded faces peering from inside, their bright eyes staring at her accusingly.

Angel shifted her eyes from them and focused her attention on the pathway towards the outhouse that loomed in the distance.

Jackson stood by the door, waiting for them. "You're late," he said, with an accusatory glance at Bren.

This was the second crime scene Jackson had come to. He'd explained the first time why he was there, but what about this time? He suspected Jackson liked Angel and was using this case as an excuse to be around her. Wasn't the morgue enough?

"Let's get started," Angel said as she pulled her gloves out of her bag and went inside.

Bren and Jackson stood silently by the doorway.

Aside from the smell, nothing else seemed out of order. Not that there was much to be out of order. It was a simple wooden outhouse that should have been condemned years ago. Other than the bench seat at the far back with a large hole to sit, it was empty.

"How did he get the body through the small hole?" Bren asked, peering over her shoulder as she took photos.

Jackson stared at him with piercing eyes while Angel lifted the lid of the bench with her boot.

"Oh."

"There were outhouses where I grew up and by my aunt's house." Angel gave him the answer before he could ask the question.

She neglected to say that this was where she grew up. He was certain she didn't want to think about it.

He listened as she rattled off the victim's details: Female, white with dark, long hair, mid- to late-forties with the same wounds as the other bodies.

She put away her camera and processed the small wooden structure.

"Do people still use this thing?" Bren asked.

"No," Jackson and Angel answered in unison.

He knew why Angel would know the answer; she could see what was with the body. But what about Jackson? Was his nose that sensitive?

Moments later, the EMT arrived and pulled the body out of the hole with lots of rope and great difficulty. No one was about to go into the hole and lift her out. The EMT checked the body and confirmed she was dead, but there really had been no doubt to begin with.

None of the bodies had looked like Angel. They had long, dark hair like hers, but the age didn't fit, making Bren wonder why the killer had chosen older women instead of those closer to Angel's age. Meredith was closer to middle age, but had said the man who visited her was interested in Angel. He knew most killers had reasons for why they did what they did, but it was never a precise science, which made it difficult to identify a specific personality or trait.

The victim lay on the floor on top of the black body bag, her eyes open and staring straight at him. He looked away.

"Anyone recognize her?" Sanchez asked.

Everyone turned towards him.

"No. Looks like another tourist, but we won't know for sure until we remove her clothing," Angel answered.

"Is there a wallet, something that identifies her?" Sanchez pushed Bren and Jackson aside so he could get a better view of the body.

One of the EMTs started to shuffle through her clothing.

Angel stopped them. "That won't be necessary." She gave Sanchez a scolding look for making the suggestion.

"What? I just thought it might help move things along faster," he said with a shrug before stepping back.

Bren watched him walk back to the barricades. He didn't like Sanchez and it wasn't just because he liked Angel, although it was a big strike against him. Sanchez was obnoxious, arrogant, and thought the world revolved around him. A bad combination for being on the police force.

"I'll get a ride with Jackson." She addressed Bren without turning to face him.

"Sure. I'll catch up with you later."

His voice and facial expression said they had a lot to talk about and that he wasn't going to let her avoid him this time. "Jackson," he said curtly before leaving them alone and making his way back to the car and then through the crowd.

As he drove to the police station, he remembered conversations he had had with Angel in college, explaining how she didn't drink. He hadn't thought about it much at the time, as her comment "I don't like to be out of control" fit her. *Did her comment mean something more?*

In the four years he had known her, he never saw her drunk, or even close, except for their one night together when she told him she loved him and then disappeared the next day. Her jaded past explained why she felt the need to keep people at a distance and he supposed it explained why she would drink. *Was her hiding the fact she drank because she was a private person, or because she was using it to medicate her issues?*

She didn't admit it, but it was written on her face that she might be having blackouts and was likely hearing voices. *Would he be able to help her? Would she let him?*

***

"You two are getting cozy." Jackson's voice cut through the awkward silence of his car.

Angel pretended not to hear him. Another two weeks had passed and still no leads. She glanced out at the passing scenery as her mind inventoried the evidence at the scene, seeking clues that might lead to whether or not she had been there. If she had committed the crime, it wasn't something she could talk to Jackson or anyone else about, just like the night she woke up and found a dead body on Meredith's bedroom floor.

"Angel?"

Jackson's raised voice dragged her focus back to the car.

"Are you okay?" His eyes were filled with worry.

"What? Yeah, I'm fine."

The intensity of his stare told her he thought she wasn't fine. *When did Jackson get to know her so well?* From the corner of her eyes, she noticed he'd changed his glasses. The rims weren't as thick and his skin had lost its usual slimy-looking sheen. He had nice skin for someone who she'd heard was supposed to be in his forties.

She shifted her position in the seat towards the door. They were passing through town and only a few yards from the police station. She wanted to shout with relief.

Jackson pulled his car up to the front of the police station and rested his hand on Angel's shoulder just as her hand reached for the handle to open the door. "Don't worry, Angel. It will be over soon."

Her heart jerked to her throat. *What did he mean by that? Did he know about her nightmares? The curse?* Searching his eyes, she saw nothing to indicate anything more than concern and a false reassurance that everything would be okay.

She gave him a feeble smile. She opened the van door and grabbed her evidence bag off the floor of the front seat.

"Thanks for the ride, Jackson."

"Anytime. I'll call you when I'm ready."

She nodded.

When she got through the second entrance, the glares she got were like daggers slicing every area of her body, even the ones that were covered. She didn't need to be psychic to know what everyone was thinking. They were thinking she was just like Meredith. For all she knew, they could be right. She'd tried to reassure herself after the second murder happened that it couldn't be her. She'd been sober, so she had control. *Was she wrong?*

She brushed the thoughts aside. *It couldn't be her.* Then why was there a horrid feeling deep in her gut? There was only one way to find out. She had to find the killer and stop him. It was the only way she'd know for sure. The only way she'd find out why.

CHAPTER 16

The moment she knocked, she wished she'd stayed at home. She had left her apartment to take a walk and before she knew it, had ended up at Bren's front door. He opened it before she could change her mind.

"Angel?"

She was grateful he didn't ask her what she was doing there. She didn't have an answer. "Can I come in?"

"Sure." He stepped aside to let her in.

She hesitated for a moment before she crept over to the couch and sat down. He watched her for several minutes, as if waiting for her to break the silence and tell him why she was there.

"What's going on, Angel?"

"What do you mean?" Even as the question left her lips, the taste of them were a bitter pill.

"Something's wrong. You're not yourself." He sat next to her on the couch.

That was an understatement. She looked into his eyes. They were eyes she'd grown to love her four years at college. Eyes that had crinkled when they shared a laugh; that had given her comfort and strength without knowing it; that had looked at her with passion and tenderness. "I think I'm the killer," she blurted.

His face registered slight surprise. "Why do you think that? Because of what your aunt said?"

He didn't believe her. Not that she could blame him. She shook her head. "Meredith was right. I hear voices, voices telling me to do horrible things. I have from the day of my eighteenth birthday."

He visibly relaxed. "There's medication for that."

"There's more." Her eyes were wide with fear at how he'd respond to what she was about to tell him. "I started having bad dreams the day of Meredith's sentencing, but lately it's been worse. I didn't think it was me because the doors were always locked in the morning, but this last time, they were unlocked. I killed those women, Bren," she whispered.

"You're hearing voices, but I don't think you're capable of murder." He rested a hand on her shoulder.

"I think I've been blacking out, at night...after drinking."

His expression was filled with concern and the assurance that he knew the answer to her trouble, and was eager to help. She wished it was more than just to fix her. The lump in her throat was difficult to swallow, but she did it and pulled herself together with what little dignity she had left.

"I shouldn't have come here."

No one could help her, and she had to remember. She had to stop trying to pull Bren into her black hole of a life.

***

Bren couldn't hide his shock when he'd opened his door to find Angel outside, looking like she'd been run over by a truck that had backed up and rolled over her again to make sure they'd finished the job. Her hair was falling from its tight grip and she was wearing sweats. Her eyes were bloodshot, as if she hadn't slept for days. She stood in the doorway, her hand clasping her handbag so tightly it caved under the pressure. He knew it wasn't another murder. She would've called for him to meet her onsite, and certainly wouldn't have shown up out of uniform. It was something else.

Bren hadn't known whether to be excited that she had come to him or feel dread over what she was going to say. It must have been bad, though, if she was not only coming to him to talk about it, but had showed up in disarray.

She'd moved inside slowly, as if deciding if she really did want to come in or run. She seemed insecure.

Her small frame had sunk heavily into the couch, as if it held the weight of the world with it. She'd gone from looking around his flat like a scared rabbit, certain someone would jump out and attack her, to a fish, her mouth opening and closing, debating what she wanted to say.

Part of him was happy she'd admitted to having a problem, but the other part dreaded the journey she had before her. He wanted to comfort her and tell her that she could stay and talk to him, but he knew she wouldn't stay.

"Let me take you home," he insisted. He hoped she hadn't driven herself over.

"No, I'm fine. I can walk," she had replied.

Walk? It was easily over two miles, even if she came by the beach. "At least let me walk you back home." He followed her to the front door. "You don't have to say anything. We can just listen to the waves of the ocean. I know you enjoy that." The sound of his brogue, along with the memories, tingled her brain.

"You remember that?" Her voice cracked.

He nodded. He hadn't forgotten a single detail about her. She loved to read. She loved Chinese food and black-and-white movies. Every one of their conversations had replayed in his mind over the years, searching for a clue as to why she'd left him after giving him the best night of his life.

She nodded. "Okay."

His hand touched her back as he led her into the hallway and locked the door of his apartment. He longed to slip his hand into hers and link their fingers, but resisted the urge. His heart was still raw from her assault and he had no intention of going through it again, even after discovering her reason. They'd been friends, no more than that, and she'd abandoned him instead of coming to him for help. That knowledge was a festering sore that pained him each time he thought about it.

Cool air brushed past them as they made their way towards the beach and turned salty when they reached the sand and strode towards the sea.

The closer they got to the waves, the more her stiff frame loosened and the hard lines on her face softened. She almost smiled. She leaned down, took off her shoes, and moved towards the water until her ankles were submerged.

He half expected her to start running and splashing her feet like a kid who discovered his feet could make water go up in the air from the joy on her face.

His heart lurched, making him wish he could join her, tackle her and drag her fully clothed into the sea and make her laugh and then sigh from his kisses.

He pushed the thoughts aside.

They remained silent the rest of the way to her apartment, the sounds of the rolling waves, the wind through the Casuarina trees, and the taste of salt on their lips keeping them company until they reached her apartment.

"Would you like to come in?" Angel asked after she unlocked the door.

An invitation inside was the last thing he had expected and was just as surprised when he answered yes. It was a bad idea, but that didn't stop him from going inside and sitting on the couch.

She stood behind her kitchen counter. "Would you like something to drink?" she asked.

He nodded.

She surprised him when she handed him a glass of milk. *All these years and she had remembered he liked drinking milk at night?*

She sat on the couch next to him, and he wondered what was going through that pretty head of hers. The redness in her eyes was gone and her hair was a mass of windblown curls around her face and down her shoulders. The lines in her face were smooth and she looked happy and positively beautiful. He'd never seen her so relaxed. He wished he'd known what a little walk along the beach could do for her. He would've flown her to a beach every weekend at college just to see that smile.

"Will you stay with me?" Angel asked quietly.

The words hung out there, making him wonder if she meant to say them, and what exactly she meant. *Stay the night and share my bed or stay to make sure I didn't leave and hurt someone?*

He told himself he was staying so that he could keep an eye on her and prove that she wasn't leaving to hurt people. But deep down he knew it was for more selfish reasons.

"If that's what you want."

To his surprise, she rested her head against his shoulder. He adjusted his position on the couch so they were more comfortable and her face rested against his chest. There were a million and one questions he wanted to ask her, but he knew it wasn't what she wanted or needed right then, so he remained silent and held her against him. He brushed her hair away from her face so he could watch as she fell asleep. It was a luxury he hadn't had their night together. Her hair was soft in his hands and several curls wrapped possessively around his fingers, reminding him she'd done the same with his heart.

The longer he watched her, the more he noticed she became restless and her face grew tortured as she slept. He wished he could see what was tormenting her. He'd never known anyone strong enough to fight off the voices that overwhelmed most schizophrenics, especially as long as she said she'd been experiencing them. He was surprised she had not fallen apart before now. He stroked her hair and she drifted back into peacefulness. She stretched and her body pressed closer against his.

His hand touched the skin on her neck. *Bad idea, man! You're already here on her couch. Now you're just torturing yourself.*

Several nights at college, she'd dozed off on the couch in his dorm room and he'd watched her sleep. Her face was softer when she slept, not guarded or stiff. He got her to smile and laugh on a few occasions, but most of the time she was serious and kept her thoughts to herself. He now knew why.

Her moaning pulled him from his thoughts. The serenity on her face was gone. Her body writhed, and her arms and legs began to make jerky movements.

"No, no! You can't make me!" she screamed.

He shook her shoulders gently. "Angel, wake up."

Her arms and legs swung wildly, nearly hitting him. He grabbed her arms firmly. "Angel, wake up!"

"NO!" Her eyes opened and looked about frantically.

She wrapped her arms around his neck and clung to him as though if she didn't, something bad would happen. Her body shook and then he felt the wetness of her tears on his shirt. He held her and stroked her back in long caresses until her breathing settled and her body stilled.

"The voices," she whispered. "They wanted me to do things." Her voice was barely a whisper, that of a child who was afraid to share a terrible secret they were hiding.

He remained silent, waiting patiently as she decided what else to tell him.

"They wanted me to kill you," she said in a quiet whisper. If she hadn't been so close, he wouldn't have heard her. "That night. That's why I left."

His pulse raced and his heart pounded while he waited for her to say more.

"I had heard them all the time, but they'd never wanted

me to kill someone before. That night we...after we fell asleep, they kept saying it again and again, and showed me these horrible visions of how I could do it. They hounded me, taunted me. I didn't want to leave, but I couldn't stay."

She clung to him, moved her face away from his damp shirt and looked up at him.

Her heart was in her eyes, vulnerable, open and his for the taking. The intensity shocked him. "Angel..."

Her mouth was on his, hot and wet, before he could say more. *You shouldn't do this!* screamed in his brain. Williams' unhappy face whirled before him, but he didn't care.

Angel would be furious when she discovered the truth, but it didn't matter. She was in his arms again. She hadn't left because she felt guilty about what had happened between them, or because she didn't feel the same way he did.

He got off the couch, lifted her, and carried her to the first door he saw, praying it was her bedroom. It was. He moved to the bed in the middle of the room and laid her down gently. Her eyes looked up at him with love, and he swore he'd do everything in his power the rest of the night to keep that love there.

He took her face in his hands and kissed her again, softly, nibbling her lips before capturing her mouth. His tongue slipped into her mouth, tasting her. She tasted of mango and something else he didn't know, but it was sweet.

He eased into the bed next to her, his lips never leaving hers and he wished he'd taken their clothes off so he could touch her naked skin and feel the heat of it against his own.

Soon.

He had all night to unwrap the gift she presented him and savor every inch of it and he intended to do just that.

Shifting away from her, he pulled his shirt over his head and threw it on the floor. He reached for her top, and pulled it over her head and was surprised that his hand was trembling. He'd waited a long time for this moment. Their one night together was branded in his mind no matter how much he'd tried to forget it, or block it with other women and his career. It haunted him in quiet moments.

Soon they were flesh to flesh and their hands ran over every inch of naked skin they could reach until they were breathless.

Her hands reached for him, urging him to the place they both wanted to go. He went there slowly, carefully, not wanting to rush her even as his heart thundered in his head and he wanted nothing more than to grip her hips and pull her to him again and again until they both cried out in joy.

"I'm not a fragile flower, Bren," she whispered hotly in his ear. It was all the urging he needed.

"I love you, Angel." The words tumbled from his mouth without his permission. He didn't care. It was what he felt and she'd deprived him of saying it when she left him. When she'd said the words, it left him in shock. He'd been reeling from her taking him home and sharing everything of herself with him, drowning with the awe of it that when she told him; no words formed in his mind to respond. He regretted it every day. He wouldn't make the same mistake.

Only silence echoed in the room. Was she awake or just pretending to sleep? He didn't care. A lot of time had passed since they had been together the last time, but the attraction was still there. He could see it in the odd times he caught her watching him.

Their involvement in the case complicated matters, but he would fix that. How would Angel act in his company now? Would she pretend nothing happened and return to her cold, withdrawn self?

Sunshine peeked through her window, cold water on their intimate moment. He eased himself out of the bed and got dressed. He didn't want to risk anyone seeing him leave her apartment. There was speculation about their relationship as it was and it might cause problems with them working on the case or his assessment of Angel. He needed to deal with that too.

He wrote a brief note and left it on the empty pillow. He caressed her face before leaving. Soon no obstacles would keep them apart.

***

Angel stretched when she opened her eyes and knew before looking over to the side where he had slept that he wasn't there. Not that they'd slept much. She smiled, remembering. She picked up the note. "Didn't want to wake you. Lunch?"

Her fingers caressed the ink of his name. She hadn't been sleeping when he'd said he loved her.

She touched her lips, remembering Bren's kisses and his hands on her body. *He loved her.* Her heart had soared with joy that he felt the same and that their years apart hadn't diminished the moments they'd shared. Once the case was closed, they could be together. She smiled, thinking about having many nights like they had had last night: walks on the beach and making love.

Cruel laughter interrupted her happy thoughts. The horrible images from her dream flickered before her.

{IYes, soon. You can't run from us forever, Angel. Think of the smooth, sticky feel of it on your hands, the metallic smell of it filling the room, and the shock in his eyes before he disappears. Hahahahah!

Angel pressed her hands against her ears to drown out the laughter, but it didn't help.

"STOP!" she shouted again and again, until the cruel, jagged laughter subsided in the distance like a song fading to the end.

It was never going to stop until she ended up like Meredith, or lived out the rest of her life in a mental institution. She was cursed. The voices were there to remind her that she couldn't love anyone, or entertain thoughts of a future with someone. Not when there was a killer lurking inside her waiting to come out and hurt the people around her, or worse, that her children could carry this burden. She couldn't take that chance. Not now, not ever!

CHAPTER 17

How could she!

After everything he was working towards—for her, for them. He wanted to smash his hand against his car windshield again and again until the cracking glass lodged itself into the knuckles of his fingers, tearing at the flesh until blood dripped from his hand, but he didn't. He longed for it to be the face of every man who'd looked at her, touched her, like the man leaving her apartment.

He hadn't given it much thought when they arrived together, because men had come before but didn't stay overnight. No one ever stayed the night. He didn't like it. The professor wasn't part of his plan, but he had to stick with the plan he'd set. The truth of it rang in his ears. It would be too risky to deviate from it now when he was so close to getting what he wanted.

The professor was nothing. It didn't matter that they had gone to college together; he was just someone for her to toy and tinker with, the way he did with the people he killed. It was him she wanted. This guy didn't know her like he did. She'd see the truth. He would make sure she knew the truth.

He played with the large manila envelope he held in his hand. It was time to play his next card.

CHAPTER 18

"I'm taking you off the case."

Angel blinked in disbelief. *Seriously?* If he'd said those words two months ago, she would've happily agreed with him, but she was too far in to be pulled out now. "Why the sudden change?"

"I'm concerned that you can no longer handle this case due to your emotional state and personal involvements," Williams stated matter-of-factly.

Shock and then the pain of betrayal shot through her as she thought of Bren. *Rat bastard!* The contents of her stomach churned, threatening to hurl to the surface as she remembered everything she'd told him about her suspicions, his assurances, and their night together. She'd practically begged him to stay. She was mortified.

I'll kill him!

"You lied to me about Bren helping with this case!"

He was just as guilty as Bren.

"I didn't lie. He was here to help and to conduct your psychiatric evaluation."

"Really? It doesn't have anything to do with these photos?" She threw the manila envelope at him.

He picked it up, and she could see his jawline tense in an attempt to not react to her rude gesture.

"Where did you get these?" he demanded.

"They were under my apartment door this morning."

He sat upright in his chair and turned away from her so she couldn't see his expression as he flipped through the photos. "Any idea who sent them?"

"No, but I suspect it's the same person who killed those people."

What was he still hiding from her? What was going through his mind? She wished he would turn around so she could see the expression on his face and in his eyes. He didn't cooperate.

"I agree," he answered.

"Are the photos real?"

Angel held her breath as he contemplated her question.

He remained silent for several moments, as if debating if he'd answer her or pretend he didn't hear her question.

"Yes. They're real," he finally said.

Angel's heartbeat ricocheted against her chest. Even though she'd seen the photos and understood what they might mean, a part of her thought he would say they were fake, or that the notion was ridiculous. That he didn't say the words opened up another avenue of possibilities and questions she didn't know if she wanted to ask.

"So it's true. You were involved with Meredith?" The words sounded foreign in her mouth.

"Yes, many years ago."

She didn't want to ask the next question, but knew it would burn a hole in her brain if she didn't.

"Are you my father?"

Her aunt had said Meredith had lied to him about him being her father, but after she'd withheld so much from her, Angel didn't know what the truth was anymore. Was that why he was taking her off the case? She was getting close to that truth. *How had he managed to keep his relationship with Meredith a secret?*

The chair creaked to and fro before he turned it around to face her. His facial expression was controlled, but she knew him well enough to notice the turmoil in his eyes.

"Did she tell you that?" he asked.

"No. She never told me who my father was."

He relaxed his stiff posture. *Was he going to deny it?*

"That makes two of us."

She shifted her weight from one leg to the other. "So all these years you didn't even suspect I was your daughter?"

"I confronted your mother, but she told me you belonged to a married man she was seeing at the same time." He linked his fingers together and studied them for a moment before meeting her gaze. "I didn't believe her, but by then she wouldn't let me near her or you."

Confronted her? No wonder Meredith responded the way she did. Meredith could be a stubborn woman, but it didn't make sense why she wanted to keep them apart.

"You had no problem getting near her when you arrested her," she provoked him.

The vein at his temple pulsed wildly. "She committed murder. I had no choice."

"You could've sent someone else."

"I needed to look in her eyes and see the truth for myself."

Then it hit her. He hadn't believed she was guilty. *Had he gone to get her, thinking she'd have an explanation?* Someone had talked privately with Meredith while another officer pulled her into the next room. She hadn't seen their face at the time. It must've been him. "What did she tell you?"

He unlinked his fingers and took a deep breath. God, she wished she could read minds.

"That she killed those people. She didn't cry, or even pretended to be sorry. I..." His voice trailed off and he shifted his position so the leather chair creaked and groaned, sounding like a ghost being tortured.

"She didn't tell you she was cursed?" Angel held her breath, waiting for his answer. If he knew about Meredith's curse, then he knew that it was hers now.

"Curse? What curse?" He sat upright.

She proceeded to tell him what her aunt had told her and Bren. Part of her wondered if he'd think she was crazy, but he had grown up in Jamaica, so the idea of a curse, Obeah, and other strange things would not seem that unusual to him.

"You think that's what happened to your mother?" he asked when she finished.

Angel nodded. Part of her wanted to tell him that she was hearing voices, but the other part remained silent. He would remove her from the force without a second thought.

"Why are you really taking me off this case?"

"You've been different since the murders started, since you visited Meredith and…"

"Professor MacDougal's assessment," she finished for him.

"You're sleeping with him."

Her eyes shot to his face.

"This is a small island, Angel."

She looked down at her hands, too embarrassed to look him in the eye.

"He didn't tell me," he answered, as if reading her mind. "You two did have a history."

"It was a long time ago, and we didn't think it was relevant to the case," she mumbled.

"It wasn't before, but now…"

"Why can't you take him off the case instead?" she prodded.

"You're both off the case."

"You need me on this case," she insisted. "The killer knows we could be related."

"We don't know for sure the killer sent those photos. And if we are related, that's yet another reason you shouldn't be on this case."

The conversation wasn't heading in the direction she wanted it to. "Meredith killed five people. That leaves two more possible victims. You're going to need all the help you can get."

His cloudy brown eyes studied her for several minutes. She held her breath while he contemplated his answer. Finally he spoke. "Alright, but you get police protection. If the killer did send you those photos, that means he's watching you. I don't need you becoming his next victim."

"I can take care of myself. Besides, if he's watching me, that means he could've killed me at any time and he hasn't. You need all the resources on this case where they belong," she said confidently.

"Fine. Make sure to keep MacDougal close," he countered.

"What? I don't need his protection."

"The protection is for him," Williams clarified. "It will also give you time to work on identifying suspects based on the profile. He might be off the case, but you can still work together."

He handed her the envelope she'd given him earlier. "Go to Jackson and have him perform the DNA test, discreetly."

Her heartbeat stuttered to a halt. Their conversation had veered off in another direction when the topic of his parentage came up and she had wondered for a second if it was on purpose. The DNA statement was deliberate and couldn't be avoided.

"Are you sure you want to find out?" She was giving him an out, even though she was praying with all her heart that he wanted to know as badly as she did. She'd been parentless for a very long time and he'd never married and didn't have kids.

"No, but we need to know."

Her heart sank. He wasn't interested in gaining a daughter. She couldn't blame him, especially given Meredith's history, and their working relationship. Bad combination. As if sensing her unease, he assured her, "Whatever the outcome, we'll face it together." She nodded, but didn't feel better.

"Right now we need to focus on getting this case solved. There are three dead bodies and no leads. I want to find this killer before he has the chance to reach number four."

She nodded. He was right. After his betrayal, she didn't like the idea of working with Bren, but they still needed his expertise. She groaned when she thought about the accusations from the other constables and their smirks.

She left Williams' office and kept her eyes fixed on the floor and walls. Anywhere but on the constables' faces. She didn't want to know what they had to say. When she reached her office, Bren was waiting for her.

"Well?" She glared at him with every furious emotion she felt.

"I was hired to assess your mental state, and to gauge if there was a possibility you were a suspect," he confessed.

She clenched her fists, trying to keep her hands from going around his neck. {I *Kill him! Kill him!* the voices chanted in her mind and for the first time she wanted to do what they were saying.

"I'm sorry, Angel. I should've told you sooner."

"You mean before you decided to sleep with me?" she said through her teeth so her voice wouldn't carry.

"Yes... I mean no...," he stammered.

She crossed her arms.

He shifted uncomfortably. "I should've told you before anything happened between us."

"From now on, think of me as you did when you first arrived, the daughter of a serial killer. That should help you control yourself."

"I thought we were past that."

"No, you got past it. I've lived with it every day of my life." She moved to open the door to let him out.

"Bring over those chemistry jammies you wore in college," she said loudly and everyone in the open-plan office stopped what they were doing. The Ice Princess was losing her cool. "It appears I'm your watchdog for the next few weeks."

Bren stood red-faced in the middle of raised eyebrows and knowing smiles. Ebanks was smiling and nudging Sanchez, who didn't look happy. Johnson looked up and shook his head as if in disgust, and then returned his attention to the paperwork on his desk.

Angel then closed her office door in his face. Her action was childish, but she wanted Bren to feel as stupid and embarrassed as she had when she found out about his reason for being there.

CHAPTER 19

Angel stared at the photo again, still in shock that Williams and Meredith had once been a couple. She hadn't intended to tell him about the photos, but when he said he was taking her off the case, she'd lost it. She'd made things worse with her reaction to Bren and then making a scene at the station. Under normal circumstances, she'd never do anything so stupid and unprofessional. But so many things were coming at her at once now; it was getting more difficult to control her responses. With shaky hands she started the car and pulled out of the parking lot of the station.

How many people knew about Meredith and Williams' relationship? *He might be her father.* The words were foreign in her mind and would be just as foreign on her lips if they became truth.

The people in the photo were strangers to her; Meredith the only one with any inkling of recognition, CS Williams smiling with his arms around her waist. *Had he loved her? Why didn't Meredith tell him the truth about her being his daughter?* There were too many questions. Questions she might never get the answers to with a murderer on the loose.

CS Williams didn't strike her as the open up and share type, and there was no hint of the smiling man in these pictures existed in him. Like Meredith, the images reflecting the happiness of the man in the pictures were long gone.

She'd thought—no, hoped—returning to Cayman would

113

simplify her life, but instead she was faced with escalating voices, a man she'd been running from for eight years, plus the possibility that her boss, and the man who had put away Meredith, her mother, could be her father. It was more than she wanted or needed in her life.

She needed a drink. At that moment, the sign for the Galleon Bay came into view, a beacon summoning her. It was a bad idea, for so many reasons, but right now she didn't care.

After parking her car, she removed her uniform shirt and put on a spare shirt she kept in her car over her undershirt. She entered the front entrance and was thankful she didn't see anyone she knew. She didn't need any condemning stares right now.

She plunked down onto a cheap wooden barstool. The bartender she had questioned the day they'd recovered the body from the hotel was working now. He was laughing with customers at the other end of the bar, entertaining them by flipping his mixers as he created their drinks. He was good, and not just his mixing moves. They were all eating out of his hands, and not just the girls. As if sensing eyes on him, he turned and smiled, flashing white teeth against gorgeous tanned skin. There was no doubt where he was spending his free time.

He sauntered over to her, making it look effortless, but she suspected he'd worked hard to perfect it.

"Well hello, beautiful. Fancy seeing you here again."

"You're not really opening with that, are you?"

He grinned. "Aye, I was. No good?"

She shook her head. "Terrible! Does that really work?"

He gave her a quick wink as his answer. "What'll you have?"

"Surprise me." Right now she didn't care what she had. She was looking for something to take her mind off everything in her personal and professional life.

He grabbed a mixer from below the counter and started

pouring different liquors into the container. After a few shakes, he poured the contents in a martini glass and placed it before her.

She didn't normally like fruity drinks, but today hadn't been a normal day. She was pleasantly surprised when she took a sip. It wasn't sweet, but tart.

He washed the containers before resting his hands on the edge of the bar. "You didn't look like the sweet drink type." His eyes raked over her face and mouth, lingering on her lips before making their way back to her eyes.

"I'm not." She played with the napkin under her glass.

He shrugged. "What can I say? I have a way with knowing people's drinks."

"Can I join you?" A man's voice greeted.

Angel groaned inwardly, wishing it was anyone but him. "Last time I checked it was a free country, Sanchez."

He smiled and took the seat next to her. "Caybrew," he ordered, not bothering to look at anyone else but her.

It was then she realized she didn't remember the bartender's name. "I'm Angel," she said when he returned with Sanchez's drink, extending her hand for him to shake.

He grinned mischievously and somehow she knew he was thinking of how to tease her. She was thankful when he didn't and said, "Jeff. Lovely to meet you, again." He kissed her hand, his lips lingering longer than appropriate, and she wondered if it was for her benefit or just to piss off Sanchez.

His eyes narrowed and his expression darkened the moment he laid them on Jeff.

"Nice to meet you, Jeff."

She pulled her hand from his and turned to face Sanchez. "What are you doing here?"

"I could ask the same of you. Returning to the scene of the crime?" Sanchez taunted.

Her eyes bore into his. The voices chanted that he would be next, and even showed her visions of her banging his face against the edge of the bar, his broken nose covered in blood, until he passed out and fell to the floor.

She suppressed the urge to smile and chuckle as wickedly as the voices in her head.

"I'm sorry. That was out of line," Sanchez said.

She relaxed slightly. Sanchez was jealous. He was one of the few constables who hadn't shunned her when she started. True, he'd gone the other way and tried to get into her pants, but she wouldn't begrudge him for that. He was a guy, plain and simple.

"Don't worry about it." She shrugged casually, as if to say his comment didn't bother her. She clinked her glass against his beer bottle. "Cheers!"

The heat of his stare burned her already tanned face and she looked down at her glass to the lime peel floating on top.

"I didn't think you drank." Sanchez turned his stool towards her.

She gave him a sideways glance. "There's a lot you don't know about me."

"I'd like to."

She shook her head. "No one wants to know me." Between the curse and Bren wanting to help her, there was no way in hell she was letting anyone near her.

"What about the professor?"

She swirled the liquid in the glass in her hand, not pausing to respond to his observation. That didn't stop him.

"You told me you were just lab partner," he said.

Angel shrugged casually. "Yeah, so?"

"Is that true?"

Her glass slammed against the top of the bar. "Why don't you get to the point, Sanchez?" she snapped.

"Did you hook up in college?"

"Hook up? Really?" she answered, avoiding his question. *What, was he twelve?*

"Well, did you?" Sanchez pressed.

She liked him better when he was trying to ask her out. The conversation was much more entertaining. "What does it matter? He's off the case."

"I heard it's because you were sleeping with him."

Great! "It's none of your damn business."

"I'm glad he's off the case. He's not good for you."

She laughed. "I suppose you're good for me," she said snidely.

"Yes, I am." His answer was so matter-of-fact, she could only tell from his expression that he was serious.

She wiped away the sweat from her glass. "Get this in your head, Sanchez. There's never going to be an us."

"I don't care about your family...history." He chose the words carefully. "That's all in the past."

She turned to face him. "That's the problem, Sanchez. It's not in the past. There's no escaping my past—it haunts me every day."

"It won't once we catch the killer," he assured her.

She shook her head. He didn't understand her meaning. It was better that way. She didn't want to explain something she didn't fully understand herself.

He covered her hand lying on the bar counter with his. "I promise we'll catch him. It won't be long now."

The expression in his eyes said he meant what he said and for a moment she wanted to believe him, but the truth was it wouldn't matter if they caught the killer or not. Her life would go on the same, cursed.

"Are we interrupting something?" Johnson and Ebanks stood behind them.

She rolled her eyes. *So much for alone time.* "No," she mumbled.

Johnson sat next to her and Ebanks next to Sanchez.

"I didn't know you drank?" Ebanks said with a grin, as if he'd uncovered some dark secret.

She didn't socialize with the officers. Not that any had

ever asked her to join them, other than Sanchez. "I don't, normally."

"I suppose the situation calls for it," Johnson said, raising his hand to capture the bartender's attention.

Her breath hitched in her throat. "What do you mean?" *Did they know about the photos of Meredith and Williams?*

Johnson lifted an eyebrow in what appeared to be amusement at her question. "Aw, people replicating your mother's murders perhaps?"

That was Johnson: polite, but direct. She let out the breath she was holding. "Yeah, right."

"How you holding up?" Ebanks asked, his expression one of genuine concern.

She felt Johnson's and Sanchez's eyes on her. She glanced between them. "I'm fine."

Ebanks' mouth opened as if to ask another question or disagree with her, but Johnson coughed loudly and Ebanks closed his mouth.

"What can I get you gentlemen?" Jeff asked.

No one had noticed him, and Angel wondered if he'd heard their conversation. She hoped not.

"Vodka and tonic for me, and another Caybrew for chubby over there," Johnson answered.

"You know the ladies love it," Ebanks replied, rubbing his belly.

Sanchez and Johnson laughed, and Angel found herself joining them. The laughter helped to ease the tension of her day and felt good.

"That's a whole lot of love," she teased. They all looked at her in surprise. "What? I can't make a joke?"

None of them responded, as if they thought answering her would break the mood. They were the handful of officers who accepted her, even with the stigma of her past. This was the first time she realized she did have people in her life and she wasn't alone. A lump of emotion lodged in her throat and tears burned her eyes. She wished she'd discovered it sooner.

Jeff returned with their drinks. "Which one of you lucky gentlemen is dating this lovely lady?" he asked.

Johnson and Ebanks looked at Jeff, then Sanchez, and then Angel, but didn't answer.

"What is this? A police reunion?"

They all turned towards Jackson. When no one answered, he asked, "Did I break up a police investigation or something?"

"Not at all," Johnson assured him.

"I saw Angel's car here, so I decided to stop in and say hi." Jackson didn't take a seat but stood behind Angel. "So what's going on?" His gaze shifted between each of them.

"Angel was just about to answer the bartender's question," Johnson said.

Jackson looked at Angel. "What question?"

"Which one of us is she dating," Ebanks answered.

The statement got Jackson's attention. His back straightened and he looked at each one of them before his eyes rested on Angel.

"None, of course," she said. "We work together."

"So that settles it then. She's mine," Jeff joked.

Johnson was the first to laugh. Ebanks, Jackson, Sanchez followed shortly after. Angel smirked at Jeff as if to imply *in his dreams* before laughing herself.

Angel stayed long enough to finish her drink before she left, despite them asking her to have another drink. She turned when she reached the doorway and studied each one of the men, memorizing their faces and the moment they shared. Sadness filled her as she realized she'd never share another one.

CHAPTER 20

Bren pulled his car up to the old house. It was hard to believe this was the same island where moments ago he'd passed a high-rise building filled with law firms and hedge fund companies.

Angel had grown up in this house after Meredith had gone to jail. It made him feel guilty for his own luxurious upbringing, filled with nannies and butlers at his beck and call.

He knocked on the door and wiped his feet on the mat.

Moments later, Angel's aunt's weathered face peeked from behind the bright door. "Wha you want?" She looked past him, as if expecting Angel to be standing by his side.

"I came here alone. Can we talk?" He flashed his best smile.

She grunted and opened the door, stepping farther inside.

The floorboards creaked as he made his way to the plastic-covered couch. The room reeked of coconut and sugar. He waited for her to offer him a seat. She didn't, merely glared at him.

"Make it quick. I na got all day."

She moved to the small stove in the corner and pulled out white and pink treats from the oven. She placed them on what he assumed was her kitchen counter.

"Can the curse be broken?" He didn't know how much he believed in it himself, but if he could find out more about her family's medical history, maybe it would help Angel.

She set her cup of coffee on the side table and sat on the couch, the plastic protesting as she got comfortable. "Wasn't you listenin' last time you was here?" she asked in a condescending tone.

He nodded.

"Her fate is sealed," Maisy said firmly.

"I can't believe there're no other options but for her to become a killer or kill herself."

Had those words really escaped his lips?

"Oh lordy! You love her!"

"Aye," he said without hesitation.

Her eyes filled with pity and then a slight smile curved her lips. "She love you?"

"She used to." *Lame answer, Bren!* It was also the truth.

Maisy stood up from the couch, went to the kitchen area, and took a pink and white treat from the cooling rack. "You want one?"

How could she think of food at a time like this? "No, thank you."

She bit into it slowly, as if savoring the flavor. She stood in the small space of the kitchen and took her time eating, making Bren wonder if it was to torture him or give herself time to think up an answer that wouldn't hurt his feelings.

"You tink you can make her love you again?" she said finally.

Bren nodded slowly.

"Good. Angel deserve happiness, even if it for a short time."

He longed to tell her the notion of a curse was ridiculous and that Angel and her mother suffered from a form of schizophrenia that could be treated with medication, but he sensed she wouldn't take him seriously.

"Is there anything else ye can tell me about your family that might help Angel?"

"Nothin' can help Angel now," Maisy said with conviction.

Looking around the room decorated with crosses and other church memorabilia, he was surprised she didn't mention prayer.

"Are there other family members I can speak with who might be able to help?" After what had happened at the station, he doubted Angel would speak to him, let alone tell him the names of her family.

Her hand paused before picking up another coconut treat. "No. Dey don't talk to or about her."

There was little to no emotion in her voice. He imagined it must be a sore point. "Has Angel ever had any contact with family other than you?"

Stern brown eyes settled on him, making him feel like he was back in Catholic school and about to be scolded by one of the sisters. "No." She didn't elaborate or explain more, but it wasn't necessary. Her earlier statement that Angel's family didn't even talk about her told him what he wanted to know.

"What do you think is going to happen on Angel's thirtieth birthday?" he asked, thinking maybe a different topic was a better option.

The kaleidoscope of emotions that moved across her face said she either hadn't thought about it, or it was the first time someone had asked her outright. "Angel is too controlled to hurt anyone, but she can't fight fate," she whispered.

Fate? He clenched his fist to control his frustration.

He stood up. "Thank you for your time."

Maisy gave him a curt nod. She walked him to the door and stood in the entryway, watching him as he pulled out the long driveway.

She honestly believed Angel would end up like the other women in her family. He wouldn't allow it to happen. Not now, not ever.

CHAPTER 21

"It's happening again, isn't it?"

Bren looked up at Williams, hoping his eyes hid the surprise he felt at Williams' question.

"Aye. The copycat seems determined to follow Meredith's murders."

"Don't take me for a fool, Professor," he warned.

"What exactly do ye think is happening again?" He didn't want to piss off Williams, but he didn't want to betray Angel's confidence either. Her secret wasn't his to share.

"She's hearing the voices, like her mother."

"Why do you think that, sir?" *He was more astute than Bren thought.*

"She didn't say it out loud, but I can see it in her eyes. It torments her the way it did her mother."

Wait? What? It sounded like he knew from personal experience.

"Was that the other reason you called me? You wanted to know if your hunch had meaning?" God, he hoped he wasn't going to ruin his hope of having a relationship with Angel over a hunch.

"I suspected the moment she returned from her visit with Meredith, but she was also so in control, not like her mother. Meredith's personality was much more carefree."

Bren studied him. *Did Williams know Meredith before her mind went to hell?*

"Do you think she's capable of murder?"

"No, but people who don't get help for schizophrenia are known to hurt themselves or others."

Bren's heart raced. "Was that why you took Angel off the case?"

"I took her off the case because of your…relationship."

Bren felt his face turning red. "I didn't let it waver my assessment," he assured him.

Williams waved away his comment. "I have no doubt of that. It's obvious you two have a past relationship you haven't found closure on." He studied Bren for several moments, making Bren wonder what he was thinking. "I know that feeling." His hard face softened. "It grabs a hold of you until you don't want to let go, can't let go for fear of losing them forever."

Where had that come from?

"Can you convince her to get help?" Williams asked in his police tone.

He decided to share the truth. "Her aunt believes it's a family curse started by one of the women in the family." He didn't give more details, not wanting Williams to think he considered it the truth.

He stared out his only office window, seeming to want to avoid eye contact with Bren. "She doesn't know what she's talking about," he answered quickly.

"I'll talk to Angel and see what I can do," Bren said.

Williams nodded. "I want to help Angel however I can."

Had that been his intention all along? Bren left the office and headed to Johnson's desk.

As he approached, Johnson looked up from a pile of paperwork. "I thought you were off the case?"

Bren grinned. "Aye, that's why I have a favor to ask."

"Fire away."

"Can you get me names and contact information for Angel's family members? I want to speak with them."

Johnson regarded him with a stiff stare, as if he'd just

asked him to give up national secrets. "Why?"

"I thought speaking with her family might shed some light on Meredith and open the door for more suspects."

Johnson digested his words. "They're probably logged in the MIR. Go check with Ebanks."

"Thank you. I really appreciate it."

"Don't thank me yet. You've still got to convince him to let you see the files." Johnson grinned briefly and then turned his attention back to his paperwork.

On the way to the MIR, Bren saw Sanchez. Bren acknowledged him with a nod and Sanchez did the same.

"I thought you were off the case?" Sanchez asked.

"I am. Just touching base with Ebanks on some last-minute information."

Sanchez crossed his arms. "He's not here today, so you can speak with me."

So much for getting the information he wanted. "Don't worry about it. I'll speak with him another day."

To Bren's surprise, Sanchez said, "I can help you."

"Okay," Bren said tentatively and followed him to the MIR.

"What do you need to know?" Sanchez asked.

"I was hoping to see the interviews with Meredith's family," he said, sensing it was better than using Angel's name.

Sanchez flipped through various files before finding what he was looking for. He pulled them out and handed them to Bren. "They can't leave this room."

Bren nodded.

"Why do you need those? No one had anything nice to say about Meredith or Angel." Sanchez sat down.

"There might be something in the files that could provide another suspect in Meredith's family."

"Really?" Sanchez asked.

"It didn't occur to you there might be someone else in the

family who had mental issues similar to Meredith's?" Bren asked, as he flipped a page of the file in his hand.

"Not really." Sanchez shuffled a few files on the desk. "I was more focused on the evidence and finding the person who had visited Meredith."

Bren looked embarrassed. "It's just a hunch."

"It's a good one," Sanchez mumbled in a tone that said he wished he'd thought of it.

Bren took a seat at the same desk as Sanchez and flipped through the files, looking for a sign of anything out of the ordinary, but there was nothing. Most either hadn't wanted to talk to the police, or were happy to share that they thought it was Angel continuing what her mother had started. He closed the last file and handed it back to Sanchez. "Thanks for your help."

"Sure," he said, and set the files down. "So, what's really going on between you and Angel?"

"It's none of your business," he said, his tone as polite as he could manage.

Sanchez smiled.

That was unexpected. Or was the smile just a façade?

"Angel is special," Sanchez said, staring him down like a criminal he was interrogating.

Bren was tempted to tell him how special he knew Angel was, and what she meant to him, but didn't. He didn't see Sanchez being that understanding, or one to take defeat lightly. He nodded before leaving the MIR.

CHAPTER 22

Angel longed to slam the door in Bren's face as he stood in her doorway. He was the last person she wanted to see.

"Can I come in?" Bren asked.

"I have nothing to say to you!"

"You had plenty to say last night, Angel," he taunted with his sexy brogue.

Her cheeks heated. *Damn him!*

He gave her a sexy grin and her stomach lurched. She hated that he could cause that kind of reaction.

"You were always a terrible liar." He pushed against the door and squeezed past her, letting himself in and ignoring her scowl.

"I lie fine! You just don't want to accept the truth." She closed the door roughly.

He closed the short distance between them, pinning her against the door. "One of us doesn't want to accept the truth, but it's not me." His breath was a soft whisper close to her lips, and she could feel the heat from his body. Her breath hitched in her throat. *How she hated him for being right!*

She pushed against his chest, avoiding the hand that attempted to hold her own. She turned to face him, arms crossed. "You pushed your way in, so what do you want?"

His eyes raked over her, making her feel as if she stood naked before him. She shifted her weight to her other foot. To her dismay, he sat on the couch and patted the seat next to him.

She gave him an "I don't think so" glare that made him chuckle. Heat filled her cheeks as she remembered the feel of his lips against hers on that same spot just hours earlier.

"I promise not to bite," he teased.

"Bren!"

He threw up his hands. "Okay, I get it." His arm rested casually on the back of the couch. "What I have to say probably requires that we keep our distance."

That was not a good sign. She held her breath as he appeared to contemplate how to start. "Say what you have to say, Bren."

He straightened his position on the couch. "Would you consider taking medication? It would help stop the voices."

"No it won't," she said quickly. She'd tried every remedy known to man, battling the side effects as she hoped and prayed each one would work. None ever had.

"You don't know that for sure."

"Yes. Yes, I do." She crossed her arms over her chest tightly. "I'm not going to subject myself to that again."

"The alternative is a better option?"

There were no options to help her. She'd tried them all and with each day that passed, the voices were closing in like the ceilings in an Indiana Jones movie.

He stood up and put his hands on her shoulders when he reached her. "I'm just trying to help, Angel."

She shrugged his hands away and took a step back. "Don't you get it, Bren? You can't help me. No one can! I have to deal with this on my own."

He closed the distance she put between them. "It doesn't have to be that way," he said softly.

She laughed harshly. "Help me? By what, becoming my first victim? Pump me full of drugs, or maybe stick around long enough to have me committed?"

"Angel." He tried to pull her into his arms, but she stepped out of his reach.

She strode to the front door. "Please leave!"

"I love you, Angel. I want to be there for you."

"Really? Then what? We get married, have kids? Do you want to risk giving your kids this curse, Bren?"

He said nothing. She knew from his expression that he hadn't thought that far ahead. She had, and had no intention of putting anyone through the pain Meredith had put her through.

"We can take it one day at a time," he said gently.

Her mocking laughter was like razorblades across flesh. "One day at a time? Haven't you heard? I have days before I go completely insane!"

"I don't care, Angel," Bren insisted and tried to touch her again.

She yanked the door open, startling a passing neighbor. "I don't want you here! I don't need anyone here!" She was shouting, and the neighbors would talk, but right now she didn't care. Her heart was breaking and she needed him gone before she changed her mind and threw herself in his arms and begged him to stay with her.

"Ange—"

"Get out!" She pushed him out the door and slammed it in his face before he could stop her or say more that might make her change her mind of what she needed to do.

She held her breath as he knocked on the door for several minutes before deciding to leave. She slid to the floor and wept into her hands until her body shook and she was choking. It was now two days before her thirtieth birthday, but right now she wished it was today so it would be over.

CHAPTER 23

The sun was setting below the golden horizon and a soft, salty breeze blew over his face. Would she come out tonight? She was a creature of habit, but with everything that had been going on lately, she wasn't herself—from skipping her morning run to not stopping for coffee. Not that he blamed her. Finding out Williams could be their father would throw anyone off their game.

To his delight, her door opened and she came out dressed in her swimsuit, a towel thrown over her shoulders.

He smiled as he watched her walk down the stairs, along the concrete sidewalk to the beach. She set her towel on the sand and made her way to the edge of the water, small waves lapping against her ankles as she looked out at the ocean.

What was she thinking? He wished he knew. *Was it him?* Surely it was. No doubt she was imagining him there with her. Whatever she was thinking, he knew it had to be about him or their future together. Soon she'd be in his arms and they could start their lives together.

She dove into the waves and it was several seconds before she surfaced and began her horizontal swim along the beach edge. He contemplated leaving his spot and getting a closer look but he decided against it. She couldn't see him from where he sat, and he could see anywhere she swam from where he sat. When she got out of the ocean and rinsed off, she'd walk right past him. It didn't matter. He'd have her the rest of their lives.

He heard his mother's laughter in his thoughts and his dreams. She'd called him a fool. She'd eat those words when Angel was at his side.

He laughed and then looked around quickly to see if anyone heard him. Only the cool night breeze and the sound of Casuarina branches knocking against each other in the wind were his audience.

His heartbeat accelerated at visions of Angel laughing in delight and throwing her arms around him and kissing him, and then they'd make love. Everything would be perfect. Soon.

CHAPTER 24

Angel pushed on the main door to enter the hospital and headed down the long corridor, a weight the size of Cayman Brac on her shoulders. Williams had asked her to speak privately with Jackson about the DNA test because he'd be discreet, but Angel still didn't like the thought of anyone knowing anything this private.

She doubted Jackson had many friends other than her, so it was unlikely he'd go blurting the news, no matter the result, with anyone. She hoped to God he was able to keep the information from being seen by others in the hospital, otherwise it was a guarantee it would find itself in the newspaper.

If she considered it seriously, she didn't really care who knew; she was more worried about how it would affect their working relationship and how it might take away from the importance of the case and finding the killer.

The last thing she needed was to be bombarded with unwanted phone calls and questions. She knew Williams didn't want that any more than she did.

She knocked on Jackson's office door.

"Come in."

He raised his head and gave her a brief smile. He closed the file, placed it in his desk drawer, and motioned for her to take a seat. "What can I do for you?"

She wrung her hands nervously before they fell at her sides. "I need a DNA test."

"Sure. For who?"

"Me," she said quickly, hoping it wouldn't result in additional questions or surprise him.

"Alright." He hid it well, but she could see the hint of surprise in his eyes.

"CS Williams said you have his DNA information on file?"

Jackson nodded, making scribbles on a notepad.

"I need you to compare them to mine, to see if we're related."

He didn't look up for several moments, but his hand had paused over his notepad. He set his pen down slowly, suggesting he was controlling his emotions before looking at her.

The control didn't last long and she could see his lips twitching to ask more questions.

"How long will it take?" she asked, hoping to distract him.

"About two weeks."

That long? She could be in a straightjacket by then or worse, in a medicated haze like the people at the institute that held Meredith. She shivered with dread.

"You okay?" Jackson's blue eyes were filled with concern. *Funny, she'd never noticed his eyes were so blue before.* "Everything okay?" he asked again.

Angel averted her eyes. *Great, he'd caught her staring.* "Yeah, fine."

It was a sad realization, but Jackson was the closest thing she had to a friend. Ebanks and Johnson were close seconds, and even Sanchez, when he wasn't trying to ask her out. She had her aunt, but she didn't consider her a friend. She was family.

She kept her eyes on the books on his shelf as he swabbed the inside of her cheek.

She nibbled on her bottom lip. "I'd really appreciate your discretion."

His expression said she hadn't needed to ask.

"Thanks, Jackson."

"Everything will work out, Angel." The comfort in his voice should've soothed her, but it didn't.

She gave him a weak smile before leaving his office.

The heaviness of her problems crushed her stomach, heart, and head with each step she took down the hallway. She avoided eye contact with everyone she passed until she finally felt the heat of the sun on her face and a light breeze blow through her hair outside the building.

The sunshine and breeze pushed back the dread, fear, and for a moment the pain and tight grip of the demons that churned her internal torment to boiling. It took sheer will to keep their taunting visions and whispers quiet.

What if Williams was her father? Then what?

Cruel laughter.

Would she have to quit her job? There were no other jobs she could do on the island with her skills, which might mean starting a new career.

Vicious laughter.

Or worse, she would have to leave the island again. *Would Williams ask her to stay?*

Rancorous laughter.

She shut the car door. "SHUT UP!"

There was a moment of silence, but before she could breathe a sigh of relief, the laughter escalated loudly, filling the small space of the car until it was deafening.

More than anything, she wanted to bang her head against the steering wheel without a care of what it would do to her hand or head, but those weren't options in the parking lot of the hospital.

She didn't know which was worse: waiting to find out if the man she'd disliked most of her young life would turn out to be her father, or wondering if she'd survive her birthday without killing someone or ending up in a mental institution.

CHAPTER 25

He had to die. There was no choice. Even with his disguise, the dim lighting, and flickering disco lights, there was a slim chance he'd recognize him, and his plan would fall apart. He couldn't let that happen.

Jeff's Jeep pulled into the afternoon traffic and he followed, ignoring the blaring horn and an angry fist waved at him out the car window. The distance between him and the Jeep was getting wider and he couldn't afford to lose track of it and its driver. Another opportunity might not come up again.

He gritted his teeth in frustration when they reached the Esterley Tibbetts Highway and double lanes. The Jeep wasted no time picking up speed and putting more distance between them. He pressed on the gas to keep up, watching the speed limit to make sure he didn't go too far over. He couldn't risk being pulled over right now.

Thankfully the bartender slowed, put on his indicator, pulled into Snug Harbor, and into the parking lot of the first set of apartments off the main road. He got out of the Jeep and went into number four. It was on the ground floor. That would make it easy. He needed to find out a few details, to make sure his plan went smoothly. He would be easy prey. He knew his schedule at work, and now where he lived.

His hands sweated in anticipation and his pulse raced with excitement at the thought of the weight of the knife and blood on his hands. He was careful to wipe all surfaces, and leave no trace behind, but sometimes he longed for the days before DNA analysis and fingerprinting, like with his first kill. No one suspected him, and there was no way for it to come back to him. It'd been perfect. He hadn't needed to worry about leaving evidence. He'd been able to splatter the blood across every surface to his heart's content and rub it on his hands, over his face, all over his body.

His excitement raised an erection and he wished Angel was his to get a release, but he knew that would be a bad idea. He would only hurt her and that was the last thing he wanted to do.

FOCUS! Don't lose control.

He closed his eyes to block out the images, and then opened them to focus on the building and then the apartment the bartender had entered. The sun was setting behind the shopping center across the road, and soon it would be dark. He drove around the neighborhood, looking for vacant houses or lots where he could park his car. He found the perfect spot, parked, and headed back to the building to review his entry and attack plan. The For Rent sign was his perfect reason for scouting the area.

He made it back to his car and he took out his binoculars.

Later, when the sun was below the horizon and the bats flew through the skies, when the roads filled with evening traffic of people heading out for a night on the town, he headed back to the building.

The complex was surprisingly silent, including inside the apartment. He'd waited until all the lights went out. The bartender was built, but he could handle him.

He took out his tools and worked silently on the back door, which was shielded by thick shrubs and trees. He entered the kitchen and made his way quietly to the door of the other room, the one he knew didn't belong to his victim.

The lump under the bed sheets told him someone was there. He approached the bed tentatively, a knife from the kitchen in hand. Hair spread over the pillow and he saw the outline of breasts under the sheets. Female. Part of him wished he'd taken care of Jeff first; then he'd have time to spend with her. He still could. He glanced over the length of her body. The moonlight streaming through the window gave him a view of her soft, feminine features and golden hair. Not brunette. *Too bad. More fun for him.* His fingers twitched with the urge to caress the softness of her curves and the feel of her muscles compressed against his palms as she struggled and he crushed her to his will.

FOCUS!

He placed his hand over her mouth and slit her throat before she had a chance to respond. Her empty, vacant eyes stared back at him, wide with surprise. He kissed her forehead and removed his hand from her mouth.

Closing her room door softly, he made his way across the hall. The sweat from his hands filled the latex gloves. Did he have family, someone who loved him? It didn't matter. He had to die.

As he got closer, he realized the room door was open. It hadn't been open when he came inside. He'd checked. *Shit! Not good.* He hated when things didn't go as he planned. He found the nearest dark wall without shadows of the moonlight and pressed his back against it. He slowed his heart rate and listened carefully for noises in the apartment. A sliver of light came from around the direction of the kitchen.

He remained still, waiting for his victim to come to him. Should he attack him in the living room or risk being seen when he made his way back to the bedroom? As the minutes stretched out, so did his patience and his anticipation.

Moments later, a figure made its way from around the corridor to the living room, each step bringing him closer to where he stood. He waited until he was inches away before grabbing him from behind. Before he could use the knife, he was elbowed in the side and flipped over thick shoulders, ending up on his back on the floor.

He used the knife to slice at the man's feet just inches from his face and smiled when curses filled the room. He jumped to his feet and punched the man's stomach and then smashed his fist into the man's face until he fell to the floor. He kicked the man in the groin and smiled in victory when he screamed. He kicked him with every ounce of strength he could muster in his foot, longing to tell him what he thought of this slimy asshole who could upset his plans with Angel, but kept silent. The scum didn't deserve words for what he did, and action spoke louder than words. He did it again and again until he was certain that he was unconscious.

He leaned down to finish him off when the door opened and light flooded the room, making him grateful he'd put a mask on to hide his face.

"What the hell?" the tall, stocky man in the doorway shouted. Three other men, not nearly as built, came in behind him. There was no way for him to take them all. He rushed back to the kitchen as they stood still in shock.

The kitchen door banged against the outside wall as he dashed out and into the dark shrubbery a few yards away. Catching his breath, he pulled off his black shirt, placed a baseball cap on his head, and shoved the shirt in the backpack he'd stashed in the bush earlier. He dashed over to the parking lot of the apartment complex a few yards away. He took more deep breaths as he raced towards the nearest car and leaned against it. He pulled out his cellphone and pretended he was having an argument with his girlfriend.

Mere seconds passed before two of the three men came rushing across the hedge that divided the apartments. "Hey, you see a guy in black pass by here?" one called to him.

He shook his head.

One of them rushed past him to the house lot next door and the other headed across the four-lane road to the shopping complex.

He finished his fake argument on the phone and took the

long route back to his car.

The car door clicked closed quietly, but more than anything he wanted to slam it shut until the window shattered. Instead, he punched the dashboard until he broke one of the air conditioning vents and his hand was bruised. *He was supposed to die!*

He was angry at his failure, but he assured himself it didn't matter. Angel would be his, and they would be long gone before anyone could suspect him of anything.

CHAPTER 26

Angel looked down at Jeff, who looked like he'd been mangled by a pack of wild animals. He was lucky to be alive.

Her heart raced with the knowledge he might know the killer. She hadn't attacked him—she knew that for certain. But it didn't ease her discomfort the way she hoped.

A groan from the bed pulled her from her mental spiral to unanswered questions.

"How you feeling?"

Stupid question, Angel! No doubt he felt as bad as he looked.

"Like hell." He groaned again as he attempted to adjust his position in the bed. He managed a smile. "I knew you couldn't resist seeing me."

Seriously? The guy was practically on his deathbed and he was making jokes? "I'm here to get evidence."

"Aye, sure you are." He flashed a sexy bruised grin.

She lifted her evidence bag for good measure. When he didn't look convinced, she placed it on the bed next to him and proceeded to take what little evidence there might be from under his fingernails.

She ignored his scrutiny as she collected the evidence from his body.

"You're even prettier up close," he whispered so close to her ear she could feel his breath on her skin.

She ignored his comment and stepped away from him,

placing what she'd collected in her bag.

"Look, I'm flattered, but this isn't going to happen," she said firmly. She was certain from his actions that he didn't know about his roommate and wondered if she should tell him.

"Why not?"

"My life is pretty complicated."

It was the truth, but this wasn't the conversation they should be having. He needed to know what had happened, but somehow she couldn't find the words.

"So you're giving me the old, 'it's me, not you' line?" His stare was level with hers.

"It's more complicated than that."

"How complicated can it be? I like you, you like me."

He took one of her hands in his. Before she could answer, Ebanks entered the room with Johnson in tow. They looked at each other when they saw Jeff holding her hand. She withdrew it quickly.

"We interrupting you two?" Ebanks asked with a grin that said, "Angel and Jeff sitting in the tree, k-i-s-s-i-n-g."

"No," she answered quickly.

"Yes," Jeff said.

She shot Jeff a warning look.

"We have questions to ask you," Johnson said coolly, pulling out his notepad.

"Can't it wait until Angel is finished with me?" Jeff said.

"I'm almost finished."

"Did you see who attacked you?" Ebanks started the questioning.

Jeff shook his head. "It was too dark, and I spent most of the time on the floor or defending myself."

"Any idea why somebody would want to kill you?"

"No. Who wouldn't love this face?" Jeff grinned.

"What about your roommate?" Johnson asked.

"What?!" His eyes darted between Ebanks and Johnson before settling on her.

"Your roommate." Johnson's eyes filled up with remorse.

"Kayla." Jeff swallowed hard. "Is she alright?"

Ebanks and Johnson looked at each other and then back at him. "You don't know?" Johnson asked.

"Know what?" Jeff's hands were gripping the bed sheets and lines of pain etched his face in anticipation of the worst.

"She's dead," Johnson said quietly.

His solid frame sunk deeper into the bed. "How?" He looked at Angel as if to ask why she hadn't said anything. She avoided his eyes.

"You sure you want to know?" Johnson said gently. He was better at dealing with victim's families than anyone.

Jeff nodded.

"Her throat was slit." Johnson placed a hand on Jeff's shoulder.

"She's me cousin," he whispered. "I convinced her to move here." His voice cracked. "I promised Aunt Carol I'd take care of her…" Tears spilled from the corners of his eyes.

Angel's heart clenched at the pain burning his face. Meredith had caused that kind of pain for the families of her victims when she killed them. Killings she had helped her with, which meant she had caused that kind of pain. The hospital room, already small with so many people in it, closed in around her.

{IYou're just like her, Angel. You killed those people too. You helped your mother kill those people.

The voices chanted again and again, getting louder each time, and coupled with cruel laughter.

"You alright, Inspector?" Johnson's eyes were filled with worry.

She cleared her throat. "I'm fine."

But she wasn't fine. Her hand ached, and she realized she was gripping the handle of her evidence bag so tightly it was cutting off the circulation to her fingers. "He's all yours." She nodded to Johnson and Ebanks and hurried from the room. She felt bad for not saying anything to Jeff, but what could she say? Nothing.

She rushed down the hallway of the hospital, her heels clicking as loudly on the tile floor as the laughter and taunting voices in her head. She got into her car, started it, and pulled out of the parking lot. She was passing the airport before she allowed the tears that were burning her eyes to fall. When her vision blurred too badly for her to see the road clearly, she pulled off by Spots Beach. Her hands started trembling and her body shook uncontrollably with pain that was ripping her apart. She screamed in anguish and banged her hands against the steering wheel until they hurt.

She hadn't told Bren the whole truth the night they'd spent together. She was hearing voices, and thought she was killing people, but the truth was she *had* killed people. Not in the same manner as Meredith, but she might as well have. She'd helped Meredith stash the bodies in the outhouse and helped her clean up the room after she killed her second victim.

No one suspected the truth. She hadn't told anyone out of fear of what would've happened to her and Meredith if she did, but mostly it was out of loyalty. Meredith was the woman who'd tucked her in at night and told her funny stories and tickled her until she nearly peed herself. Meredith had been different for months and Angel had felt in her heart there was a reason why those people had died. She'd clung to the hope that killing would make her mother return to her happy frame of mind. But it never did.

It was only when she was in the courtroom that she realized what Meredith had really done. What she had made her do.

{IYou can't escape us, Angel.

They were right. They'd tormented her the moment she turned eighteen. She'd known from the first moment she

143

heard them she was like her mother, but didn't want to tell anyone. She'd been scared she'd hurt others, but was more terrified by what they'd do to her if anyone found out the truth.

She strived to control herself and everything in her life, believing she could contain the evil inside her, that she was stronger than her mother, but she was a fool.

The pain and suffering she saw in Jeff's eyes haunted her the way the faces of the victims' families had all those years ago. There was no escaping her fate. She had to take matters into her own hands.

CHAPTER 27

Angel took a deep breath and steadied her hands before entering the police station. Williams had asked for an update, and Ebanks and Sanchez were putting together the evidence from all the cases, along with the bartender's statement. The next murder could take place at any moment, and they still had no clues as to the identity of the killer. The hope that Jeff could provide a lead was a sore disappointment everyone felt.

The piercing stares of every constable burned her. She could single-handedly catch the killer and drag him behind her car down the middle of George Town and people would still be wary of her because of what her mother did twenty years ago.

She nodded politely to those constables she passed who had the courage to look at her.

That morning she'd woken up in a cold sweat, right before she slit Bren's throat with her mother by her side urging her on, along with the other voices that were always in her head. {I *He can't love you the way we do*, they'd taunted. They'd be with her the rest of her life and there was nothing Bren, drugs, or anything or anyone else could do. She'd wished and prayed since she'd first heard the voices and nothing had changed. Not then, not now, not ever.

She swallowed the lump of pain threatening to choke her and blinked away the tears burning the back of her eyes. Everywhere she looked she saw death, blood, pain. Everyone she walked past was someone who needed to be hurt, stabbed, or killed. The voices were so loud they blocked out all the other noises around her, escalating higher and higher with each person she came in contact with.

Coming into work had been a bad idea. She should've called in sick. But when CS Williams called her in, she knew she wanted to see him one last time.

She headed to the bathroom and splashed water on her face. She jumped and nearly screamed when she saw Meredith's face staring back at her.

{IYou can't escape me, Angel.

She squeezed her eyes shut, willing the image to disappear, but it was there waiting for her when she opened her eyes. Her fingers dug into the porcelain sink and she put her head down until she was staring at the muddy colored tiles on the floor. *It's not real,* she said again and again, until she heard the bathroom door open. She stood up quickly, pretending to fix her hair.

"CS Williams is looking for you," a female constable said when she saw her. "He's in the MIR."

Angel gave her a half smile.

The constable backed out of the bathroom, as if she were afraid Angel might attack her.

She took a deep breath and shook her hands to stop them from trembling. She left the bathroom and went down the hall to the MIR.

She stuck her head inside the room. "CS Williams, can I talk to you privately for a minute?"

"Sure." He stood up and together they walked to his office.

"Everything okay?" he asked when the door closed.

"No." She went to sit in one of the chairs in front of his desk.

To her surprise, he took the seat next to her and put his hand on her shoulder. "What is it?"

"I'm hearing voices. Like my mother," she said quietly.

"I know, Angel." He removed his hand from her shoulder.

"What?" That wasn't the response she expected. "How'd you know that?"

"I suspected." He shifted the chair so he was facing her. "I was there when they started for your mother. I saw how hearing the voices tore her apart. You're always so in control of your emotions, but the last couple weeks, you've been different."

She placed her face in her hands and wished she could weep, but here wasn't the time or place. "I just want it to stop."

"I know."

He surprised her again by putting his arms around her and she longed to put her head on his shoulder, and for it all to go away.

"There are medications," he said tentatively.

"They don't help."

"Have you spoken to Bren about it?" he urged.

"He thinks he can help, but no doctors can help me. I went to them all when I was in London. Nothing worked." She shifted her position in the chair.

"I'm sorry."

She was grateful for those simple words, that he didn't try to convince her the way Bren had. His words made her feel better than she had in weeks.

"What happened to my mother, towards the end?" She didn't really want to know, but she needed to know.

"I was only there when it started. She was different. Our last night together, I woke up to find her standing over me with a knife in her hand and a look I'll never forget on her face." He paused. "She told me she never wanted to see me again, ever."

As he talked through the rest of her mother's words, about

how she didn't want him or anyone else in her life, Angel couldn't help but feel as if she were reliving her mother's life—even with everything she'd done to try to avoid repeating the same mistakes. For the first time, she understood her mother and regretted how things had ended between them at the institution.

"Why didn't you try to find out if I was your daughter after my mother was sent away?"

He leaned back in the chair. "I tried to, but your aunt convinced me it was better that she raise you."

"And you let her?" Pain that he may have abandoned her pierced her heart.

He nodded. "It was a complicated time in my life."

"Complicated?"

Was he serious? What did he think was happening in her life?

"Your mother was gone—I'd been the one to put her away. How would it look if I suddenly claimed you as my daughter?" he reasoned.

Angel pushed her chair away from him. "Do you have any idea what it was like for me? If not for my aunt, I might have ended up on the streets!"

"Do you think my family would have been any better?" he said quietly. "I'd just been promoted. I wouldn't have been able to give you the time and attention you needed and there was no way I would find someone to take care of you."

She stood up and paced before him. "You couldn't have visited me? Let me know I wasn't alone?"

"You weren't alone. You had your aunt," he assured her, as if that would make her feel better. *The hell it did!*

"I was alone!"

He reached for her hand when she came closer, but she pulled it away. "Think about it, Angel. How confusing would it have been for you if I suddenly showed up saying I was your father? Me, the man who'd put your mother away for life," he said gently.

She continued to pace as his words sunk in. She stomped her foot. He was right, damn him, but that didn't make her feel better. For years, each night before she went to sleep, she'd wished he'd end up covered in warts. It would've been a cruel joke for him to end up being her father. In a way, it still was.

"You're the reason I went to college," she said when the realization hit her. When her scholarship was approved, she'd figured they wanted to get her off the island, a dirty secret they didn't want to see or know anymore. "And the reason I got this job." So much for thinking he didn't want her hired.

"Yes, for the college, but no for the job. I didn't think it was a good idea for us to work together, especially if there was a chance you were my daughter."

She laughed. She couldn't help herself.

This time she didn't move her hand away when he reached for it.

"It's going to be okay, Angel," he assured her in a fatherly tone.

She longed to believe him, but they both knew the truth. She might not end up killing people as her mother had, but her life would change.

"I can arrange for full-time patrol, to keep you safe if the killer decides to come after you."

She laughed again. "We don't have the resources, and the press would have a field day if you did. Besides, it would pull away from the resources you need to find the murderer. At least we know where the next murder will take place, if not the time."

He nodded. "You'd think on an island this small, someone would see something."

"They don't want to see. They all think I'm guilty and should be arrested and put away like Meredith was."

"Are you going to be okay?"

"I honestly don't know. Tomorrow is my birthday and it's supposed to get worse."

149

"Worse? How much worse can it get?"

"My mother committed her first murder on her thirtieth birthday," she said quietly. "I remember her waking me up to help her clean up the room."

She looked up at the man who might be her father and found no judgment in his eyes. *What would he have done if he'd found that out twenty years ago? Would he have put her away too?*

"Your mother never let you out of her sight, but I never dreamed she would involve you that way. I'm so sorry, Angel."

"It's okay. By then she wasn't my mother anymore. She did all the things for me she had before, but I knew in my heart something was wrong. She wasn't herself." Those words cut through her heart like a butcher's cleaver chopping through a beautifully frosted cake, making it a mess.

"I should've been there for you." His voice was thick with guilt.

"No, you were right," she assured him. "I would've hated you if you turned out to be my father then."

Pain filled his eyes. "And now?"

She gazed down on his dark hands that held hers as if she were the ten-year-old girl he'd interviewed all those years ago. It hadn't been easy working with him in the beginning, but she'd come to know him as an honest and reliable man. "Now, I won't mind so much."

He squeezed her hand for good measure and she longed to wrap her arms around him.

"So what now?" Angel asked like a lost child.

"We have a meeting with the team in five minutes."

A brisk knock on the door interrupted them, and they put distance between themselves before Ebanks and Sanchez came in.

"Everyone's waiting for you," Sanchez said.

She stood up and headed towards the MIR. She never

considered herself a coward, but the more she thought about it, the more she realized she had only one option.

Inside the MIR, Johnson and other officers working the case were already there. She went to stand next to Williams at the front of the room. More chairs had been moved in and the tables that normally occupied the middle of the room lined all the walls. A projector sat on the small table next to Williams. He started it and the first round of images came up.

"We know for certain the killer is copying Meredith Mason's murders, so what's stopping us from catching this guy?" Williams glanced at every officer in the room. No one answered.

"Are we still patrolling Meredith's murder sites?" Angel asked.

"Yes," Sanchez replied. "But we only have so many officers available to work around the clock."

"And the neighborhoods are so thick with houses, anybody could come and go and we wouldn't see 'em," Ebanks added.

"I want to hear solutions, not problems," Williams countered.

All the officers murmured and nodded in agreement, although Angel suspected that they all had the same feeling. Unlike Meredith, this killer would be difficult to capture.

Each officer provided their update on the area of the case they were responsible for. At the end of the meeting, Williams dismissed them and most of the officers left the room. She stayed behind and looked around the room with the heaviness this might be the last time she was here.

"Want to tell me about it?" Johnson asked. She hadn't heard him approach.

She shook her head.

"That usually helps me." His warm voice washed over her, soothing her sadness.

Somehow she couldn't imagine Johnson sharing

anything personal about himself. Like her, he usually kept things professional. The bar was the first time she'd heard him laugh.

"You're a nice man and a fine officer, Johnson," she found herself saying.

Johnson's eyebrows furrowed as if he expected her to grow horns. "Come again? Now you're truly worrying me."

She managed a light smile. "You won't have to worry about me much longer."

He didn't have time to ask her what she meant. She squeezed his hand and raced from the room, the feel of his eyes following her.

CHAPTER 28

When she returned to her office, Sanchez was waiting for her.

"Let me take you out for your birthday."

No "Do you have plans?" or "Can I take you out?" Not like that would make a difference. "No thanks."

"Come on. I'll make it worth your while."

She rolled her eyes. The man needed a course, maybe two, in manners. "I'm sure you would, but as I said, I'm not interested."

His hands gripped her arms from behind and he pulled her frame against his.

{IKill him, kill him. He deserves it! Cackle, cackle!

Great, now he was resorting to brute force? She was seriously considering the voices' suggestions. She yanked her arms from his grasp and turned to face him.

"I'm sure most women would be flattered by your interest, Sanchez, but I'm not one of them."

He ran a tanned hand through his wavy black hair. "You were interested in the professor."

She moved behind her desk and sat down. "That's really none of your business."

"What's he got that I don't have?"

Manners was the first word to come to mind. She decided on, "It has nothing to do with you."

He jammed his hand into his pants pockets. "You're

using the 'it's not you, it's me' line on me? I practically invented that line."

She didn't doubt it. "Look, Sanchez, you're just not my type."

He stalked up to her desk and placed his hands firmly on the surface, glaring at her. "I'm everyone's type," he insisted.

"Would you listen to yourself? You're arrogant, obnoxious, and downright rude. Does that sound like my type?"

"But I love you."

Those weren't words she had expected to come out of his mouth. "You don't love me. I'm probably the first woman who's told you 'no.' You just want me because you can't have me."

"That's not true." He reached across the desk and took her hand. "I knew I wanted you the moment I laid eyes on you. You're beautiful, intelligent, and sweet, despite coming off as a hard-ass."

His sincerity shocked her. Her harsh resolve softened. "I'm flattered, but this isn't a good time for me." That was the understatement of the year.

"Why?"

"It's complicated." She couldn't tell him the truth.

"Is it because of the professor?"

"No," she said quickly.

"Then what?"

"I've got a lot going on in my life right now, Sanchez."

He walked around the side of her desk, his hand still clasping hers. "Let me help you through it." He said it so tenderly, and with such sincerity, she found it hard to believe it was the same man from moments earlier.

She patted his hand. "I appreciate it, but it's something I need—no, have to do alone."

From his expression, she knew he didn't understand. She didn't expect him to any more than she expected Bren to.

Before she could remove her hand from Sanchez's grasp, Bren strode into her office without knocking. His gaze went to her and then Sanchez before settling on their clasped hands. She pulled her hands from Sanchez quickly, but from the fire in Bren's eyes, the damage had already been done.

"I'll talk to you soon, Angel." Sanchez addressed her informally and for the first time, she didn't give him a corrective glare. "My offer stands," he said gently.

She nodded. It was better not to answer when she saw Bren's jawline twitch. "Thanks, Sanchez."

The door closed behind him and the heat of Bren's scrutiny filled the room and scorched her skin with its intensity.

"What offer?"

No mincing words for Bren. Even though she had told him to go to hell, she knew him well enough to know he wouldn't listen. "He wanted to take me out for my birthday tomorrow."

He visibly relaxed. "Are you alright?" It was a rhetorical question.

"Better than I expected, all things considered." It was an easy lie and better than telling him about the voices telling her to kill him where he stood.

He placed his hand on her shoulder and her pulse raced, drowning out the echo of the voices. If only breaking the curse was that simple, she'd stay in his arms forever. She took a step back, pretending not to see his hurt expression.

"Better is good."

She didn't respond, her heart still racing as she remembered their night together. What she wouldn't give to spend another night with him, but he wasn't hers to have. Her throat tightened at the thought of another woman in Bren's arms, holding his children, and growing old with him.

She cleared her throat and shuffled the papers on the surface of her desk to distract from her pain. Cruel laughter erupted. She longed to squeeze her eyes to shut out the noise, but knew that would get Bren's attention and the last thing she wanted was his pity. She knew he thought it was schizophrenia, but she knew in her gut it wasn't. With each year that passed, with no drug being able to help, she knew it was something more and that it was her cross to bear.

"What do you want, Bren?"

"It's your birthday tomorrow," he said simply.

Unlike Sanchez who offered to take her out or spend it with her celebrating, he was offering his company for other reasons. "Okay," she said to her and Bren's surprise.

He closed the distance between them. "I'll come by at eight with Chinese," he said with a slight smile. For a moment, they could imagine it would be just another night of them eating Chinese and watching a movie, like they did in college. "See you then."

He gave her a crooked grin and left her alone in the office.

{lKill Bren! Kill Bren! echoed in the room after he left, leaving her to wonder if she'd made a huge mistake accepting his invitation.

CHAPTER 29

Angel glanced at the clock when her doorbell rang. Seven o'clock. It couldn't be Bren. She looked through the peephole. To her surprise, Jackson was standing in the hallway. She opened the door. "Jackson? What are you doing here?"

"Can I come in?"

She stepped out of the doorway. "Sure."

"It's different than I imagined," he said as he circled her apartment.

Was that a good thing, or bad? "How did you imagine it?"

"More pictures of your mother." He kept his back to her as he glanced at the one photo she had framed on the table behind her couch. "Is that the professor?"

"Yes."

"I didn't realize you were…friends." He chose the words carefully. No doubt he'd heard about their relationship.

"I don't have any photos of Meredith." She went around his question about Bren. Not that talking about Meredith was any better.

"Why not?"

Seriously? He needed to ask that question?

"I didn't want any memories, not even happy ones." The joke was on her. Not having photos hadn't mattered. Meredith—the good, bad, and ugly—were branded in her mind whether she wanted them there or not.

157

"That's a shame."

"Can I get you something to drink?" she asked, hoping he'd take her hint to change the subject.

"Um, yeah, sure. Got any beer?"

Jackson was a typical guy after all. Somehow she didn't imagine him as a beer drinker. "No, sorry."

"Did you know I was in Cayman when your mother's case was in court?"

"Really?" *Why didn't that surprise her?* Even then he was interested in dead bodies.

"Yes. It was a pretty big deal back then."

It was a pretty big deal today, but he was right: twenty years ago it was worse.

"I couldn't believe it when I saw you coming out of the courtroom after she was sentenced. I didn't think they'd let kids in there, even if she was your mother."

Why the hell was he continuing to talk about her mother? "My aunt insisted I be there when she was sentenced since there was a chance it'd be the last time I'd see her."

"You looked so lost and sad," he said quietly, as if caught up in a memory of his own. "I wanted to tell you everything would be okay."

The hairs on her neck stood to attention as she remembered Meredith's comment about the visitor being obsessed with her. She tried to push aside where her thoughts were going, but found herself remembering all the conversations in the morgue—his fascination with the bodies and what had happened, and then his showing up at the crime scenes. At first, she thought it was Jackson wanting to help her because of Meredith's connection to the cases, but was it something else? As she explored all the possibilities, blood rushed to her head until it felt like it would explode.

It was then she noticed he was wearing a cream-colored silk shirt with the top two buttons undone, revealing a patch of dark hair. The tightness of the shirt revealed he was more athletic than his usually loose clothes showed. His hair was different too. Instead of looking like a cheap wig, it was nicely styled and flattered his face. She sensed that if he removed his glasses, he'd be quite attractive. Not that she ever thought he was ugly, just a little strange. Standing this close to him, she could see he had beautiful eyes behind his black-rimmed glasses. His face wasn't as greasy looking and he actually looked like he'd been out in the sun.

He looked completely different. Alarms went off in her head. *Is that how the killer was able to go unnoticed?* The killer had to coax those women to be alone in their hotel room with a stranger, someone they'd just met. On a normal day, she couldn't see Jackson coaxing anyone anywhere, but this man? Yes.

Jackson was one of the few people in her life she considered a friend, but the truth was, she didn't know anything about him other than his profession and that he had spent his summers in Cayman with his parents as a child. He was brooding and solemn, and she just assumed it was part of his personality. But did his serious demeanor hide something sinister?

"When you transferred to Cayman's police force, I knew we'd be working together." He gave her a dazzling smile.

She didn't ever remember seeing him smile that way before. It changed his face, making him incredibly sexy. The way his eyes raked over her was unnerving, and gave her tingles like when an attractive man looked at a woman with appreciation.

What the heck happened to the Jackson she knew? The shy, timid man who barely looked her in the eyes and blushed if she stared at him for too long? This man was a different creature altogether. He was Sanchez and Bren rolled into one and on steroids.

"When we started working together, I realized we had so much in common and I wanted to get to know you better." His soft gaze studied her.

159

What the hell did they have in common? She searched her memories of their conversations, but couldn't remember anything specific. She always sensed he liked her, but he never did anything about it, which was fine with her. Recently he had been different. She couldn't put her finger on it, but he asked her personal questions, seemed more confident, and wanted to be part of the cases when it wasn't necessary.

Oh my God! He's the killer! The notion sliced through her thoughts. The air to her lungs stopped, as well as the blood to her heart. Her hand squeezed around the cold glass beer bottle as she tried to get her fear under control. She placed her hand on the kitchen counter.

Breathe, Angel!

He squeezed her arm. "Are you okay?"

She couldn't read his expression, and wished to God she could read minds. "I'm fine," she assured him. "Why are you here, Jackson?" She watched his face as he contemplated her question.

"I think you know I'm crazy about you," he said tentatively. "I never said anything because I knew you weren't ready for a relationship. I watched, waiting and hoping."

He watched her? Her stomach lurched that her suspicions might be right.

"Then the professor came into the picture and complicated matters." His brows furrowed and he stuck his hands into his pants pocket. "It was obvious you liked each other, and I had my own personal hiccup."

Hiccup? She didn't like the sound of that. *Was it murder?*

"I've cared about you a long time, Angel, and knew I needed to do something or I'd live with regret."

Something? Beads of perspiration formed under her arms and her legs began trembling as she waited for him to tell her that he was the killer and she was his next victim.

He took off his glasses, folded them, and placed them in

his pants pocket.

She was right. He did look better without them. Her heart was hammering so loudly she was certain it would burst from her chest.

"I'm going to kiss you," Jackson whispered.

Wait, what? What the hell kind of killer was he?

She looked up at him and chills ran through her at the intensity and the anticipation, hope, love, and fear that swirled behind his eyes. *He wasn't the killer.* Relief came over her like a tidal wave just as his lips met hers, and she was pressed against his lean frame. His mouth devoured hers, coaxing her lips to open under his heated assault. She couldn't help but respond; the kiss was really good. Who knew shy Jackson knew how to use those lips and his tongue for something other than talking about work or dead bodies?

{IKill him! It would be so easy. He's so trusting.

She pushed against him, breaking his embrace. His hands rested on her shoulders.

"So there's no chance for us? For me?"

"I'm sorry, Jackson, but things are just too complicated right now."

"We all have issues, Angel." His tone was low and pensive.

"Not like this."

"What is it?"

She nibbled on her bottom lip in thought.

"Are you having the same problems with schizophrenia as your mother did?" he asked in his doctor tone. "There's medication for that."

Did everyone know about her hearing voices? After tomorrow, it wouldn't matter. They'd all find out the truth, but she'd be gone.

"My mother had more than schizophrenia," she murmured. "Besides, I've tried all the medications there are and they haven't helped."

"You're not a killer, Angel," he said softly.

"You sound like Bren," she said, annoyed. It was easy for them to say; they didn't hear the voices or feel the strong tug of the thrill of the kill they offered, or the rampant emotional roller coaster of guilt and torment.

"He's right."

"Maybe, but it doesn't really help me." Her voice broke.

Jackson pulled her into his arms and the strength of her tears beat at the back of her eyes. *Get it under control, Angel, before you lose it completely!*

"My mother died when I was ten," he whispered. "My father couldn't handle it and I became the parent for many years. It was hard, but we got past it." His eyes met hers. "That day I saw you come out of the courthouse, you had the same look I'd seen in my own eyes for years. I know it's not the same situation, Angel, but I promise you it gets better." His hand was stroking her hair and it soothed her.

God, how she wished she could believe him, but despair squeezed out any hope. *Should she tell him what she was planning?* The words died in her throat. His friendship was one thing she'd miss and didn't realize it until that moment. "Thank you for your friendship, Jackson."

He studied her for several seconds before he spoke. "It's been a pleasure, Angel."

A knock on the door saved them from an awkward moment of silence.

She answered the door and Bren entered.

"Professor," Jackson said.

{ITwo victims, two victims! The voices filled the deafening silence.

"Jackson?" Disbelief washed over Bren's face as he gave Jackson a once-over.

"I was just leaving," Jackson said.

Jackson took her hand in his and kissed it softly. "Don't worry about me, Angel. Kissing you made me realize there's somewhere else I should be."

She pulled her hand from his. "Night, Jackson."

"Professor."

Jackson closed the door behind him, leaving Angel alone with Bren. Her body hummed with excitement from being alone with him, and dread at how the voices would taunt her with hurting him in some way. "It seems I'm popular today."

He smiled. "That reminds me." He pulled a small box from his pants pocket and placed it before her.

For a moment, it felt like her heart stopped but then sped up again. The box was black and velvety, the same kind of box that held jewelry, very small pieces of jewelry. She reached for it with trembling hands and opened it as if something unpleasant would jump out and bite her nose.

She grinned when she saw the contents. It was a silver bracelet, and a bright green frog with orange eyes hung from the middle of it. She adored frogs. It was one more thing he had remembered about her. It made her heart ache that she wouldn't be sharing more memories with him.

Bren pulled the bracelet out of the box and wrapped it around her wrist.

"Thank you," she said.

The heat from his hand on her wrist scorched her as did the way he watched, like a man whose prize was just out of reach and he wouldn't be happy if he didn't get it.

She pulled her hand from his grasp. "I need your help, Bren."

"Anything."

His lack of hesitation warmed her heart and made her wish all the more she could spend her life with him instead of doing what she had to do. "Take me to the airport tomorrow so I can fly out to the Priory Hospital in Hayes Grove."

He couldn't hide his relief. "I'll do one better. I'll go with you."

He had never said the words out loud, but he must have

been thinking about it for some time. "Thanks, Bren. That means a lot to me."

He took her hand and led her over to the couch. "This is for the best, Angel. This way I can keep an eye on you and oversee the care you get to make sure the medication is the best and not ones you've already gone through. I will be there with you every step of the way."

Did he think she'd want him there as she went crazy? He must be the crazy one. "It wasn't an invitation for you to take care of me, Bren. I only want you to take me to the airport. I don't want you to check me in, or work with the doctors there."

"But I thought—"

"You thought wrong, Bren."

"Angel, please."

"I want you to remember me this way, not after…" She pleaded with her eyes for him to leave her with a little bit of dignity.

He looked ready to argue with her, but then seemed to change his mind. He nodded.

"Thank you." She knew that her rejection hurt him, but this way was better.

"I'd do anything for you, Angel."

He stood before her, his heart in his hand, ready to offer it like a sacrifice to her even if it meant he'd get nothing from her in return but a few stolen moments to reminisce before she was gone forever. Pain and regret pressed against her, sucking the air out of the room and her lungs. She longed for more time and wished she'd taken it with him in college instead of wasting the four years they had keeping her feelings for him hidden, hoping, praying he would be the one to share his feelings and put her out of her misery. But no, she'd squandered it.

She closed the distance between them, wrapped her arms around him, and kissed him with every emotion she'd felt the moment she'd laid eyes on him. His arms wrapped around her, kissing her back with as much intensity, his tongue delving into her mouth, soft and sweet, conquering every last bit of her that she'd denied him. His hands went to her face and deepened the kiss, saying with the kiss everything he'd wanted to say to her from the moment they'd met. They clung to each other for the future they wouldn't have together and uncertainty of what lay ahead.

When they parted, Bren caressed away her tears with his thumb and he kissed her on the forehead. She rested her face into his shoulder and inhaled his scent, willing her mind to remember it no matter what happened. His lips lingered on her head and they stayed there, holding onto each other as if it would make a difference. As if nothing bad would happen if they stayed in their embrace.

Harsh laughter erupted in her mind, loud and unwanted.

{IIt's time to kill, Angel.

CHAPTER 30

Wind rustled through the tall trees overhead, blowing tamarind and almond leaves in a whirlwind around her car as she drove up the driveway to her aunt's house. Her aunt had called earlier that day to apologize and asked if she was coming over for her birthday. It was a tradition for them to spend the day together, but they settled on dinner instead.

She parked the car and made her way up to the sand yard and smiled when she looked down at the new cheery welcome mat outside the front door. Aunt Maisy always had a new welcome mat, even when the house crumbled around her inside and out. Angel had helped out whenever she could, but the house was showing its age in a way nothing but a bulldozer could fix.

She knocked on the door and went inside when she heard her aunt beckon her.

Her aunt wrapped her plump frame around her own thin one. "Happy birthday, child."

"Thanks." Angel looked down at the woman who'd been her caretaker as a child, the only family that remained after her mother was hauled away. She'd been so angry when she found out about the secrets Maisy had kept, but she was the only family she had.

"Is Dustin Williams my father?" she asked.

Maisy paused on the way to the plastic-covered couch and turned to face Angel. "He told you that?"

"No. Someone left an envelope at my doorstep with photos of him with Meredith. I asked him about it."

"Wha he said?" She eased her frame unto the couch so carefully Angel wondered if she was in pain.

"That he didn't know. Meredith never told him."

Did she keep the truth from her for the same reasons Dustin had, or was it because of the curse? She hadn't liked his side of the story, but she understood it. She hoped the same was true of her aunt's reasons.

"He say anyting else?"

Angel relayed their conversation, watching her aunt's face for signs that she could be lying or trying to spare her feelings, but her face revealed nothing.

Her frame relaxed into the couch, making it squeal in protest. "Dustin was right. The truth would only hurt you."

Angel clenched her fists at her side. "That might have been the case when I was a child, but what about when I got older? I had the right to know!" she protested.

"Know wha?" Her aunt straightened her back. "That your daddy was the man you'd hated your entire childhood? Wha if he wasn't your daddy? Wha that would do to your relationship? Wha if he was?" She crossed her legs. "Wha then?"

Angel remained silent, the sting of her aunt's betrayal still fresh in her mind. Her whole life, people had lied to her. Whether for good reasons or not, it didn't make it easier to swallow or take the sting away.

Maisy held out a plate of coconut tarts she picked up from the glass coffee table. Angel gave her a small smile. Coconut tarts were her comfort food as a child. She took one.

"Did Dustin say anyting else?" Maisy asked, putting the plate back down on the coffee table.

"No." *What more could there be?* That he could be her father was shocking enough.

A knock on the door interrupted them.

Maisy lifted her heavy frame from the couch and shuffled to the door. "Wha you doing here?"

"Let me in, Mother. I know she's here."

Mother? Her aunt didn't have any children. Another lie. The voice sounded familiar but she couldn't place it.

"No. I don want you here."

Chuckling came from the doorway, but it wasn't friendly. Angel stood up slowly. No one but Bren knew she was there.

Fearful anticipation was a loud drum in her ears and the cackling, taunting voices the musicians. Each one escalated with each step that took her closer to the doorway.

His face came into view, but she still couldn't believe what her eyes were telling her. Even the voices in her head went silent. The shock blocked out all noises in the room, muffling the arguing.

All their times together were a broken record replaying in her mind as she searched her memories for some sign he'd ever tried to tell her the truth, but there was none.

Her stomach lurched, remembering how he'd pursued her as a romantic partner. He was her cousin.

CHAPTER 31

The front door banging shut rattled the windows and Angel. Sound returned like a tidal wave, drowning out the silence. Muffled voices turned into shouting voices—her aunt's.

His face was calm and his voice level as he spoke. "Hello, Angel."

"Hello, Sanchez." Her voice was thick with disbelief.

Maisy put both hands on her plump hips and glared at him. "You needa leave!"

His eyes didn't leave her. "And I told you, I wasn't leaving, Mother." Malice lurked beneath his tone.

"You don belong here," Maisy insisted.

"I'm not here for you. I'm here for Angel."

Angel didn't know why he was there to get her and at the moment she didn't care. There was only one answer she wanted. "How is my aunt your mother?"

"Dat don concern you, Angel," her aunt replied for him. The words hurt. *When would the lies stop?*

"She had an affair with my father—who was married," Sanchez answered.

Her uptight, church-going aunt had a child with a married man?

Her words, "You're lying" got drowned out by her aunt saying, "Don believe him, Angel."

Angel stared at Sanchez and then at her aunt. She didn't know who to believe.

"You knew we're related and you still wanted a relationship?" Revulsion ran up her spine.

"She's not your aunt," Sanchez said calmly.

The words were an atomic bomb exploding into an already toxic atmosphere. Angel took deep breaths to steady her racing heart and ignore the voices' high-pitched cackling. She longed to rip her hair out to stop them—something, anything—but nothing was an option. Not now.

"That's a lie!" Maisy insisted.

His laughter rang through the room. "Okay, so that one is not really true. But let's face it. Your mother gave birth to you while your father was away at sea." His caramel eyes taunted Maisy.

Angel didn't bother mentioning that still made them related. At this point, she didn't think it mattered to him.

"Is that why you did it? You couldn't stand people thinking you, Miss Upstanding Citizen, are a bastard child?" Sanchez asked.

Maisy's face appeared to expand with the urge to scream at him, but her mouth remained closed.

"It's amazing what people will share when you're a police constable. You find out all kinds of information, especially when people don't know who you are."

He grasped Angel's hands before she could pull them out of his reach. "Did you know it was your dear auntie who started this curse?"

The sensation of a freight train barreling off track crashed into her with such force her knees buckled beneath her. Sanchez caught her before she fell to the floor.

Her eyes shot to her aunt and then back at him. "You're lying!"

Maisy's eyes narrowed, contorting her face to a dangerous expression.

It couldn't be true! The words reverberated in her mind again and again. Maisy had raised her, been the only family she had when her mother was taken away and no father was in sight. She'd held her while she cried herself to sleep the first two years after her mother was sentenced. She was the one who'd made sure she did her homework, brushed her teeth, and defended her when the kids in the neighborhood had picked on her.

It didn't make any sense. She couldn't have cared for her the way she did knowing she was the cause of her pain. *Could she?*

"You put a curse on your own sister because of a man and then did the same to her daughter just for spite."

"Shut up!" Maisy's hands were fisted so tightly Angel was certain she was drawing blood. "You don know wha you talking about!"

Angel looked at her aunt, and then Sanchez. Both were people she thought she could trust, but right now she didn't know who to believe. The voices in her head that were laughing as the scene unfolded started chanting in high-pitched tones.

{IKill them both! Kill them both!

"NO!"

Sanchez and Maisy looked at her, thinking she was talking to them.

"Who's the man?" Angel asked, gaining control.

"Dustin Williams," Sanchez answered.

Emotions and questions bombarded her mind as she struggled to control them. "I thought he was with Meredith?" Angel asked.

"He was mine first!" The hatred in her aunt's voice surprised her.

"Why would Meredith do that?" She knew nothing about Meredith and CS Williams' relationship other than what he had told her.

171

"Because she could."

Maisy released her clenched fists. The lines in her aunt's face narrowed, becoming sharp edges. *How had she missed this side of her all these years?*

"I thought the curse started with your grandmother?"

"I told you that to hide the truth."

She kept her eyes on her aunt as she moved about the small room.

"I knew a woman from Jamaica who agreed to help me— for a price, of course. All the darkness of my hate and anger towards his"— she pointed her chin at Sanchez—"father and Dustin went into your mother. It was the perfect revenge." Maisy's laughter was harsher than the voices in Angel's head. "I didn't think your mother would actually kill anyone—just go mad. That was a nice extra. You know how hard it was not to smile at her sentencing?"

Angel's stomach convulsed at the callousness of Maisy's words and past action. She searched her memories for that day in the courtroom, but she had no memories of anyone but her mother and trying to get her attention. People could've been acting out a comedy in the back of the courtroom. She wouldn't have noticed. Her world was crumbling around her, and the one person she loved in the whole world was being ripped from it and didn't seem to care.

Raw emotions washed over her in waves at the realization that her aunt, a woman she loved, had ruined her family and life.

"Break it now!" Angel shouted.

Maisy chuckled cruelly. "Why should I?"

"Because of the relationship we have. Because I'm your niece and you care about me. Pick one."

"And give you a chance at happiness when mine was taken away?" Her eyes locked with Angel's. "Never!"

Bile rose to the back of her throat, pain pierced through her body, and her aunt's words shattered the tiny hope she'd clung to. The rage churning inside her erupted and she closed the distance between her and Maisy. Her hands went around her aunt's neck faster than Maisy could step out of reach.

Triumph glimmered in Maisy's eyes even as Angel squeezed her neck tighter. Her eyes bulged and her mouth opened slightly as if trying to gasp for air, but she stayed silent, her cloudy brown eyes daring Angel to kill her.

{IKill! Kill! Yes, squeeze her neck harder—until there's no breath left.

For several seconds she listened to the voices and smiled when she saw the life leave Maisy's mocking stare: her eyes dead and her body slumped to a heap on the wooden floor.

{IHa, ha, yes, yes! The words rang victorious in her mind.

An image of Bren's face broke through the fog of images the voices had built around her. His eyes were filled with disappointment. She released Maisy's plump neck instantly. Angel was relieved when she heard Maisy gasping for air and heard her harsh laughter ringing in between gasps of air and coughing. "I'm not a killer!"

Maisy raised her plump frame from the floor. The top of her head barely reached Angel's chin. *How could such a small woman cause so much trouble?*

"You're just like your mother. A bad seed." Her voice was low. She braced her hands on her knees as she continued to catch her breath.

Angel squeezed her hands shut, the nails biting into her palms to keep them from reaching for Maisy again. "You're the bad seed! You disowned your only child, then cursed your own sister and her child. You took care of me and led me to believe you cared about me!" She choked as the pain lodged in her throat. "Why?"

"What would people have thought if I didn't?"

She stared at Maisy in disbelief. *That's why she did it?* She was concerned about what people would think of her?

173

"Perfect Miss Maisy taking in her murdering sister's kid, was that it?" Her laugh was humorless.

"I've heard enough!" Sanchez interrupted.

Both women looked in his direction, forgetting his presence.

"You've done nothing but cause the people in your life pain. People you should've loved and taken care of," he spat. He stood between Angel and Maisy, his back facing Angel, protecting her.

"This ends today," he said to Maisy, pulling on her arm. "I won't have you causing the woman I love any more pain."

The tension between Maisy and Sanchez was thick enough to hack with a machete.

Maisy snorted. "The woman you love?"

"Yes. The woman I love and intend to marry." His dangerous stare bore into Maisy.

"Wait just a minut—"

Angel didn't get a chance to finish. Sanchez pulled a gun from the back of his pants. Both women stared at him in shock.

"Sanchez. I don't think—"

"Let me handle this, Angel." He cocked the gun, placing his finger on the trigger. "If she dies, the curse will be broken."

Would it? It wasn't a risk she was willing to take.

"What if you're wrong?"

He looked sideways at her. "I'm right." The confidence in his voice didn't waver as he continued. "The moment I found out about her and the curse, I knew she had to die." He flashed her one of his dynamite smiles. "Just as those women had to die."

Coldness settled in the pit of her stomach and then she had the sensation of it sinking to her feet; she was certain it would be lying on the floor in pieces if she looked down. *He killed them?!*

"How could you? You're supposed to protect people. Not kill them!" Her voice escalated the angrier she got. She jerked her hand from him. "Why?" Her breath hitched in her throat as she waited for his answer.

"You needed to know that your past didn't matter to me, and I needed to prove to you that I would do anything for you."

Oh my God! He was serious. He was deranged! All their time together on cases, especially this one, played out in scenes in her mind. At no point did he ever give any indication he could do such a thing. He was arrogant and pushy, but never in a million years would she have pegged him as a killer. She was suffocating from all the lies around her.

"They were innocent women, Sanchez!" she insisted.

His eyebrows narrowed in confusion as though he didn't understand. "Of course they were innocent. That was the point. I studied your mother's cases to get everything right. She was a master, the way she was able to incapacitate those men. I was lucky enough to have the strength she didn't, but I wanted everything to be perfect. To show you I was worthy of your love. That I knew you and your family better than anyone and it wouldn't make a difference to me. I want you, Angel. I've always wanted you."

He lowered the gun for a moment and stepped towards her, the tenderness in his eyes at odds with the dangerous weapon in his hand.

"It started out as revenge against Maisy for abandoning me and leaving me in the hands of my stepmother. Did you know she used to beat me and lock me in the closet for days without food?" The question was directed at Maisy.

"Your father wanted to raise you," Maisy argued, but there was no regret or apology in her eyes.

"He was never there and his wife"—he spat the words—"made sure I knew every minute of every day that I didn't belong in their family."

175

He turned his attention back to Angel. "When I found out about Maisy's curse, I knew it wasn't a coincidence. I visited your mother, and then watched you in England. The loneliness in your eyes captured me, and I knew that I wanted you for myself: To comfort you, care for you, and love you."

Under normal circumstances, any sane woman would welcome—heck, be thrilled—to hear those words. This wasn't one of those times. She opened her mouth to speak, but what could she say? If she said the wrong words, she could end up just like the women he killed. She pressed her lips together.

His gun lifted again at the sound of the floor creaking as Maisy attempted to move out of his range. "Going somewhere, Mother?"

"You won't get away with this." Maisy's voice pierced through the silence.

Sanchez's head fell back as he roared with laughter. "Of course I can get away with it. Who's going to suspect me?" He shifted his footing and his grip on the gun. "You're going to be the next victim of the copycat killer."

Maisy's eyes widened. "But, I'm your mother," she stammered.

His eyes narrowed to slits. "You've never been a mother to me, Maisy. You didn't show me love or that you even cared for me. You hid me like a dirty secret and sent me away!"

"I had to! There was no other choice." Maisy tried to reason with him, but to no avail.

"Shut up!" The veins at his neck bulged and his Adam's apple contracted. "There's always a choice."

His eyes closed and he took deep breaths. The tenderness in his eyes returned as they fell on Angel. "So now you know the truth."

Angel's mind raced with options, but none came. She was overwhelmed with the news: being related to Sanchez, that he was the copycat killer, that he planned to kill Maisy—her aunt and his mother. *What was his plan for her?*

176

"What now?" Angel asked. He'd said he loved her. *What would happen if she rejected him again?*

He gave her a dazzling smile before pulling the trigger of the gun, sending a bullet right between Maisy's eyes. A silencer muffled the sound of the shot.

A scream died in Angel's throat as her aunt's plump form crashed unto the wooden floor, the planks rattling. Her gaze shifted to Sanchez; his face shone with delight, his eyes on Maisy's dead frame. She needed to find a way out of this situation and quick.

In London, it'd been easy to deal with criminals. It wasn't personal. This was different. This was Sanchez. The co-worker she'd sat next to during briefings for the past two years. The man who'd brought her lunch and asked her out. Would she have seen what he was if she'd paid closer attention to the signs instead of being caught up in her personal problems? Could she have saved the lives of those women?

"Now that you're free, we can be together," he said calmly, as if discussing the weather, or where they'd go for dinner.

"You shot her!" She avoided the topic. She combed every corner of her mind for signs the voices were gone for good. Silence echoed in her mind, but that was no guarantee.

"It might raise a few eyebrows, but I plan to dump the body in the cistern, so there'll be some similarities." Sanchez shrugged. "Serial killers change their MO all the time."

"How to you plan to get away with this?"

She couldn't ask what she really wanted to, afraid of his answer. *How was he going to keep her silent?*

He put the gun in the back of his pants and held out his hand for her. "It was never my intention to keep killing, Angel. I got my revenge on Maisy, and I have you. With no more murders and no leads, the case will go cold."

She gave him her back and moved towards the couch to

put distance between them. Holding his hand was a vile thought she didn't want to think about, much less do.

"I don't love you," Angel whispered, thinking of Bren.

"That will come with time," he said confidently, as if he had an answer to all her concerns.

"My feelings towards you haven't changed all this time," she pointed out.

Not a good idea, Angel.

"That will change with all the quality time we'll be spending together."

He chased her around the room, not seeming to notice that she was avoiding him.

"We don't have much time, Angel. We've got to get rid of Maisy's body so we can start our new lives together."

His words "get rid of Maisy's body" echoed in her mind. *He couldn't be thinking that she'd help him?* Visions of helping her mother deal with the first victims were burned into her memory and she didn't want to enhance them with a new one. The other bodies had been hard enough to forget, and she hadn't known those people. How hard would it be to forget someone she knew? Maisy wasn't just anyone: she had raised her, been a big and important part of her life, even with the betrayal. "I can't," Angel whimpered.

Sanchez sighed loudly. "I know it's hard, but we have to do this together. It's the only way I know you won't tell anyone. You were part of it, helped me do it."

Tears beat at the back of her eyes, desperate to come out. She couldn't let them, not now. "I can't, Sanchez. Please don't make me do this."

He took her hand in his. His thumb wiped away a stray tear she hadn't been able to contain. "It's going to be okay."

That was the problem. It wasn't going to be okay, would never be okay, even with him getting rid of her aunt. She had no idea what he had planned for her after this. Her mind raced in too many directions to track them at the possibilities that awaited once Maisy's body was disposed of.

Sanchez's large hand covered her mouth and his strong arms imprisoned her. She struggled against him, but there was only so long she could hold her breath. Soon the room blurred; all noises disappeared. Darkness flooded the spaces filled with light, and then her mind, before there was nothing.

CHAPTER 32

Angel woke to a pounding headache and winced when she opened her eyes. Her surroundings were blurred and she struggled to bring them into focus. She placed her hands on her temples and rubbed them, hoping to ease the ache as she adjusted her body.

Metal rattled in the distance. She concentrated harder to see around her, ignoring her throbbing brain.

The room was painted a cheerful blue, the color of the sky. Clouds floated through it, along with parrots and other local birds. On the wall behind her were the ocean and the setting sun. The paintings were so vivid she could almost smell the salt of the sea and feel the sun on her face. Looking around the rest of the room, she saw a small door in the corner and a beautiful king-sized bed.

Then the memory of what had happen in her aunt's house played before her. *Out! She needed to get out and now!*

Was she in Sanchez's house? *It couldn't be.* There were no windows other than those painted on the wall with views of scenes in Cayman.

Dread loomed over her like a weakly secured piano. It was a lovely room and space, but a prison nonetheless. She remembered a case of a woman being held by her captor for several years before anyone found her. She became his wife and mother of his children, but against her will. As much as she valued her life, a quick death was starting to look good.

Bile rose in her throat at the thought of sharing a bed with Sanchez and then bearing his children. It didn't matter that he was charming and good-looking. She knew what he was capable of and even if they weren't related, he wasn't someone she wanted to spend her life with. Bren's face popped into her mind. He was the one she wanted.

She choked back the tears that she might never see him again. He'd said he wanted to be with her, even despite all her issues, and she'd rejected him. She was a fool. How many people wished they had someone to stand by them in difficult times? He had offered his devotion to her on a silver platter and she had pushed it away like it was last week's leftovers. Would she be here now if she hadn't been so stubborn?

The sound of a door opening pulled her from her thoughts. She looked around the room for something she could use as a weapon. There was nothing. There was no way she could overpower Sanchez. He was a black belt in karate, something he bragged about. She hadn't even taken a class. She knew how to defend herself against criminals if things got hairy, but a fellow constable? There was nothing about that in the police handbook.

She took deep breaths to soothe her racing heart and moved as calmly as shaking legs could take her into the room where Sanchez entered.

"What the hell's going on, Sanchez? What am I doing here?"

He grinned. "Glad to see you're up and around." He took her hand in his when he was near her.

She pulled it from his reach.

He chuckled. "Don't be angry. This was the only way to get you here. You wouldn't have come if I'd asked."

"This is ridiculous! You can't keep me here forever!"

"I don't intend to. Once things are safe, we'll be heading by boat to Honduras to start our new life," he said with a smile.

"People are going to wonder where I am," she said quietly.

"Don't worry, honey. I've got that covered." He took her hands in his large ones. She didn't move them away. "People will think you killed your aunt and then disappeared. I set it all up. We'll be free to be together."

"What about you?"

He shrugged. "I plan to go on with business as usual. Everything is planned out perfectly. You don't need to worry about a thing. I've taken care of it," he assured her.

He hadn't revealed anything. *Now what, Angel?* She didn't even know where she was. He was too smart to keep her within earshot of anyone.

His hand stroking her arm brought her back to the room.

"Make yourself pretty. I'll be back in an hour. We'll eat and then start our new lives." His hand moved from her arm to caress her face and he leaned in to kiss her.

She turned her head away.

His hand dropped. "You need time. Once you see how much I love you, you'll understand this is for the best."

For the best? He was deranged! This could never be for the best. She wanted to scream. Instead, she looked down at her hands, certain he'd see her hatred and fear if she looked him in the eyes. She didn't want him to see either.

"There's clothes in the suitcase." He pointed with his chin towards the bed.

He left her alone in the room and she heard more than one bolt lock the door. She went towards the bed. Sure enough, there was a black suitcase on the floor.

The last thing she wanted was to play games with Sanchez, but it wasn't a game. Maisy was dead and she was his prisoner who'd be on her way to Honduras only God knew when. Until she came up with a plan to escape, she needed to stay alive.

She opened the case and rummaged through it. There was

nothing but dresses and the underwear was frill and lace. She never wore dresses and only liked cotton. She gritted her teeth. There were no sweatpants, shorts, or even a T-shirt. *Did he think she was going to prance around in those silly things all day?* The hell she would! She slammed down the lid. It was then she heard the whirling sound.

Oh great. A camera? She should've known. Sanchez was that sick and twisted he'd want to watch her squirm, among other things. She had no intention of giving him a show. She'd stop bathing if she had to. Maybe if she stunk badly he wouldn't want to touch her. She realized that was futile. He'd gone through great lengths to pull off this elaborate scheme. She doubted a little body odor would stop him.

Part of her longed to defy him and not get dressed, and tell him to go to hell, but she'd seen the exhilaration in his eyes when he'd killed his aunt. He was no typical stalker. Most killed as a means to an end, not because they enjoyed it. He had enjoyed killing his mother, and she had no doubt that he'd enjoyed killing those women. They'd been easy prey for him. His charm and good looks were an intoxicating scent meant to attract their kill. She had no intention of ending up like them.

CHAPTER 33

"What the hell do you mean she disappeared?" Williams roared from the other end of the phone. "You were supposed to be watching her!"

"Don't you think I know that?!"

When he woke up, he realized Angel hadn't come back from her aunt's. She hadn't called and her phone was going to voicemail. He'd called the police station to see if she'd stopped there, but she hadn't. He waited at her apartment as the time for her flight came and went before he called Williams to tell him what a piss-poor job he'd done of watching Angel. "I should've gone with her to Maisy's."

"You shouldn't have let her out of your sight," Williams insisted.

"She wanted time alone with her aunt to say goodbye."

"Goodbye?"

"She was going to check herself in to the Priory Hospital and we were scheduled to leave on a flight early this morning."

"Why the hell didn't you tell me?"

"It wasn't my place to tell you, sir." Angel hadn't said the words, but he imagined she would've called Williams once she reached the facility to let him know. "She was worried you'd try to talk her out of it."

Williams' silence told him she was right.

"Meet me at Maisy's house in ten minutes. I'll get Sanchez and Johnson to meet us there."

Bren hit the End Call button on the phone and headed out of Angel's apartment. His mind raced with unanswered questions as he drove to Maisy's. *Had the killer followed her there? Had Angel been his final victim?* Sharp pain pierced his heart with the thought that Angel could be dead and gone from his life forever. He pushed the thoughts aside.

When she left him all those years ago, he'd been hurt and angry, but he should've followed her. Even after he knew the truth about her family history, he should've gone to her and told her how he felt. He'd been scared that she'd reject him again.

She had told him she loved him and he'd laid there like a river stone, cold and hard. *Is that why she pushed him away?* She didn't want their kids to be cursed like her. Didn't she know that he would give up wanting to have kids for her? He'd have given up anything to share his life with her, but he hadn't told her that.

Regret stabbed at him. He shouldn't have left her alone last night. He should've stayed with her until they got on the plane.

He was thankful when Williams pulled down Maisy's sandy driveway at the same time so he wouldn't have to wait for him to arrive. He got out of the car and darted to the front door, Williams close behind. He knocked on the door, hopeful Angel was still there, despite wanting to kick it down and charge in.

There was complete silence. Not even the sound of music from the local radio station, like he'd heard on his other visits, could be heard from behind the door. His chest tingled and his fingers grew cold even in the blazing heat as he knocked again.

When there was still no answer, he reached for the door handle with trembling hands and turned it. It opened easily.

He wrinkled his nose at the smell that greeted it when he stepped inside Maisy's house. There was no body in sight, but something was off.

Williams' weathered face was etched with worry. "Check that side of the house. I'll check the other," he stated in a tone much calmer than he looked. "Don't touch anything! Sanchez and Johnson will be here shortly."

Bren nodded and opened the door to the next room. Maisy's bedroom. It was small, with only room for a small twin-sized bed and a dresser. The closet had no door, and an assortment of church dresses and house dresses hung inside like skeletons.

There was one photo of Maisy and Angel standing together at what he assumed was her high school graduation. Although it was a happy day, neither was smiling or appeared happy. Only a solemn line graced each of their full lips.

Had this been her life growing up? When he met her aunt, he'd gotten the impression that she cared for Angel, but there were no other pictures of her around the house or other reminiscences of their lives together. His parents had pictures of him all through school and even kept things like horrible clay sculptures he'd made in art class for them.

His shoulders dropped as he imagined how lonely her childhood had been and how difficult it must've been for her to accept what he offered her. It wasn't just about the curse. She'd been alone most of her life, unable to rely on the people she loved. Her own mother had let her down and she had no father to take care of her, love her—to show her that people could be depended on.

When he got back to the living room, he found Williams standing over dried stains on the floor.

"Is that blood?" Bren asked.

"I'm pretty sure it is, but there's no body in the house." He paused and looked up at Bren. "The next victim was found in a cistern, right?"

Both men rushed out the front door and to the side of the house to the cistern. Bren's heart hammered in his chest with each step. He stayed back, letting Williams go in first. He told himself it was because he was the police, but part of him knew it was fear. Fear of what awaited them beneath the crumbling wooden cover. Palms sweating and hands shaking, Bren stood behind Williams and watched as he lifted the lid and looked inside.

Below them Maisy floated, her plump face turned up towards them and her eyes wide in surprise, as if asking them what happened.

Williams placed his hands on the side of the structure, as if catching his breath, before his back straightened. He turned to Bren.

"She's not there," Williams confirmed.

Bren could only nod.

"Maisy doesn't fit the profile, so why was she killed?" Williams asked.

"Killers are known to change their MOs."

"It's obvious this killer was following Meredith's case to the letter, so why change his victim type now?" Williams turned to make his way back into the house. "He kept the location the same, but it doesn't make sense why he targeted Maisy, unless it was part of his plan. But why?"

Bren was glad he didn't mention that Angel might be the final victim, a possibility that had begun to plague him following the relief that her body was not in the cistern with Maisy's. *Did that mean they had two more weeks?* He pushed the unpleasant thought aside.

"Maybe the murders had nothing to do with Meredith, but Angel. Meredith said her visitor was obsessed with Angel," Bren said, realizing it still didn't answer the question about Maisy.

"Maybe Maisy was in his way?" Williams offered.

Bren shook his head. "No, this killer is too intelligent for that. Everything up to this point was carefully planned. He wouldn't change that now. We just need to figure out how poor Maisy fit into his plan."

They looked about the living room one more time for a clue of why Maisy had been chosen and what happened to Angel.

"There's nothing here to tell us what happened to Angel," Williams said finally. "Let's check her apartment." He headed towards the door.

"I was there just this morning," Bren argued.

"We should check it again, just to make sure. There could be leads."

They found Johnson outside the front door waiting for them when they exited, along with Sanchez.

Williams briefed them both on Angel's disappearance and what was found inside Maisy's house.

"Get started here and call me if anything turns up," Williams replied. "We're heading to Angel's apartment."

"Yes sir," both constables said in unison.

The sound of other cars passing was the only noise in the car as they rode to Angel's apartment. The weight of her disappearance, and now her aunt's death, hung heavy in the air.

Bren prayed, something he hadn't done in years, that Angel was there safe and just dealing with a schizoid episode, but a thought hit him like a ton of bricks, knocking the breath out of him. *Did Angel kill her aunt in a schizophrenic haze?* Angel herself had said she was having blackouts. Had this been one of her episodes?

NO! He refused to believe it. She'd been falling apart, but she still had enough control to refuse his offer of a future together. She had the internal strength to control herself from hurting someone.

Once they arrived, Bren stood by as Williams knocked loudly on Angel's apartment door. After standing outside for several moments and knocking two more times, Bren went to find the property manager to let them in.

The petite woman with flamboyant short hair and clothes

opened the door reluctantly. "Angel's not going to like this," she insisted.

"When was the last time you saw her?" Williams asked, ignoring her comment.

"Yesterday morning."

"Did she say where she was going?"

"No. Why would she? What the heck is going on?" she asked, looking from Bren to Williams.

"She didn't show up for work and no one's seen her since yesterday," Bren answered.

"You think the man who killed those women got to her?"

"We can't answer that question," Williams replied.

"But—"

"Thanks for your help." He gave her a polite smile before closing the door firmly in her face.

Bren held his breath as he waited for direction from Williams.

"Take this side. I'll take the other," he finally instructed.

Bren gave Williams a quick nod and headed to Angel's bedroom and bathroom, looking for clues that she'd taken off or had been taken against her will—anything that looked out of place. There was nothing. He didn't know whether to be relieved or to worry more. He hoped to God Williams was having better luck than him.

His eyes gazed over Angel's made bed. His heart swelled with joy and pain as he remembered their night together. He wished he could go back to that night and hold her a little longer, kiss her, and tell her how he felt without the pain of the past blocking him.

"Find anything?" Williams asked from the doorway.

"No, nothing out of the ordinary," Bren said, stepping away from the bed. "What about you?"

"Nothing. If he took her, it was probably from Maisy's."

Damn! Bren raked a hand through his hair. *Had that been his plan all along, to take Angel? If so, then why kill those women first? Why not just take her?* He scanned the room once more before heading back to the living room.

"She kept your picture," Williams commented, picking up the photo of them from college.

"Aye. It surprised me too.

"What happened?" Williams asked as he placed the picture back on the table.

Bren studied his face. *Did he want to tell him what happened?* It wasn't something he wanted to share with anyone, especially him. "We weren't compatible."

"And now?"

Two weeks ago, Williams wouldn't have asked him that question. *Did he think Bren took her?* Either way, he knew it was better to be honest with him. "She doesn't see us having a future together because of the curse."

The intensity of Williams' stare bore into him, making him feel like a suspect being interrogated.

"How did that make you feel?"

What the hell? Bren wanted to slam a fist into his face that he was wasting time instead of trying to find Angel. "Shouldn't we be looking for Angel?"

Williams looked past him to the front door before he answered. "Where do you suggest we start?"

"How the bloody hell should I know? That's your job!"

"Does Angel's disappearance make you angry?"

Bren jammed his hands in to his pockets to keep from punching something. *Of course he was angry Angel had disappeared.* "Stop psychoanalyzing me."

"I'm not," he insisted.

Williams seemed to study him for several seconds before speaking again. "There's nothing here," he said and turned to Bren. "I'm heading back to the station. Come with me."

Bren obliged. He knew time was running out—that the next twenty-four hours, now less, were crucial to finding Angel before her captor decided if he didn't want or need her alive.

CHAPTER 34

Angel looked down at her bare legs and her hands that lay folded and shaking in her lap. Twenty minutes earlier, romantic eighties music had come through the speaker system. He really had studied her to know that much detail about her life. He must have been in her apartment and rummaged through her things. Her stomach jerked. *Had he been there when she was alone? Sleeping? Passed out drunk?*

It still hadn't registered for her that she and Sanchez were related in a weird way and that she was now his prisoner being held God knows where. She wanted a drink and bad. She was wearing a summer dress, for crying out loud!

She leaned into the leather loveseat.

It wouldn't have mattered. He'd planned this out for a long time. Her hand went to her throat. *What next?* Part of her didn't want to know. The other part wanted to know every detail so she knew what to expect so she could prepare herself mentally and physically. *Was this how victims felt?* She didn't like it.

The sound of chain rattling in the distance made her fidget and adjust the hem of her dress so it covered more of her thighs. Her heartbeat drowned out the music as she watched the door, waiting for Sanchez to walk through.

The knob turned slowly. Once opened, the door cast shadows on the wood floor, small at first and then longer as the door opened wider.

She expected him to walk in quickly and close the door behind him, afraid she might try to make a run for it. The fact that he didn't said he was either tormenting her or had every confidence he could keep her captive.

"Good evening, Angel."

She heard his voice before she saw him. He held roses in his arms, along with a bottle of wine and a couple of plastic glasses. Dressed in a crimson silk shirt and black pants, he looked like he was out to impress. It didn't matter to her if he was dressed in a tuxedo and carrying diamonds; she didn't want him anywhere near her.

"Hello, Sanchez." She said his name with enough chill to freeze hell.

Not thwarted, he smiled at her.

He swiftly closed the distance between them, placing the bouquet on the table before her. He didn't wait for a thank-you but opened the wine with a corkscrew he took out of his pants pocket.

After pulling the cork, he filled two glasses and handed her one.

"A toast," he said, and raised his glass to touch hers. "To us."

Their glasses clunked together before she could protest. *Us.* She wanted to vomit.

She waited until he took a drink before pretending to take a small sip herself.

"I can't marry you, Sanchez."

He smiled brightly as if not hearing her words. "Of course you can. We obviously can't have a minister, but I can do it."

That wasn't what she meant, but she didn't try to correct him. She took a long gulp of the wine, letting it linger on her tongue, savoring it. It wasn't vodka, but it was better than nothing. Would he leave the bottle behind? She hoped so. She'd need it no matter how the night ended.

She emptied her wine and reached for the bottle.

"You shouldn't drink so much." He frowned.

"We all have our vices, Sanchez."

He motioned towards the bottle of wine as if to take it away, but drew back. "It was just for revenge and to get your attention," he assured her.

Yeah, and I only drink when I'm stressed. "I saw the look on your face, Sanchez."

"I know how to control myself."

"I don't—"

His voice raised an octave. "Don't argue with me, Angel."

She opened her mouth to speak again, but decided against it.

"No one knows you have a drinking problem." His eyes bore into her. "Not even Bren."

She shifted uncomfortably.

"When I saw him leave your apartment that morning, I thought you wanted him instead of me." His hand squeezed around his wine glass until his knuckles whitened. "But you refused him like all the other men in your life."

She'd rejected him too, but she wasn't going to point that out.

"I knew you didn't want anyone but me."

Man, he really did have screws loose.

"Sanchez," she said.

He set down his wine and reached for her hand. She tried to pull it away, but she wasn't fast enough. He pulled her hand to his lips and she glanced towards the coffee table where the corkscrew lay. He hadn't bothered to engage all the chains on the door. If she stabbed his hand hard enough with the corkscrew, she might make it to the door. Her limbs trembled and her chest ached as the scene played out in her mind. Sanchez was no lightweight.

She scanned his tall, athletic frame. He wouldn't go

193

down easy. As badly as she wanted to get out of here, she had to keep her head on if she wanted to make it out alive. She shuddered as she remembered the sinister grin on his face when he shot Maisy. No weapons were in this space, but that wouldn't stop him from squeezing the life out of her with his bare hands.

His hand rested on her leg and she pushed it away.

"You don't strike me as coy, Angel." He laughed and his eyes twinkled.

"You don't know that side of me," she shot back.

His voice softened and he leaned closer to her until she could smell his musky cologne. "I know all the things you do when you think you're alone. I know all your fantasies." His arm was behind her and the more she leaned away from him, the closer he came. His hand gripped her bare thigh.

At that, she elbowed him in the ribs and smashed his face with the back of her hand. She grabbed the corkscrew from the table, stabbed him in the thigh, and then jumped off the couch and raced to the door, not looking back, knowing it would slow her down. The sound of Sanchez's cries of pain and curses echoed behind her.

Her fingers touched the door handle. *Please give me more time* chanted in slow motion in her mind as she yanked the door open. Her heart soared when she stepped over the door frame. Blackness engulfed her, and she put her arms before her, groping for anything to guide her. She screamed in pain and frustration when the tight grip of arms went around her waist, pulling her backwards.

She struggled against him. Her arms and legs swung frantically as she tried to inflict more pain and gain her freedom. Sanchez locked his arms around her, tighter and harder, until her ribs and lungs protested. He dragged her back to the room and threw her roughly to the floor. She scrambled up to attack Sanchez again, or at the very least make another run for it, but he hit her across the face. Not enough to make her see stars, but it hurt like hell. Her skin burned and her jaw ached.

"Is this the thanks I get?" Sanchez shouted. "After everything I did for us to be together, you try to leave me!"

Gone were the charming smile and warm eyes that had graced his face when he'd come into her prison earlier. Pure anger was etched there now, making him more dangerous. He grabbed her by the hair and dragged her across the floor to the room with the bed.

The word "NO!" formed in her mind, but didn't make it to her lips—the pain of her hair being pulled from the root silenced her. He threw her onto the bed, the force of her body shifting the bed out of place.

"You can't ever leave, Angel. You belong to me. We belong together," he bellowed.

"No, we don't," she said firmly.

"Stop saying that!" He placed his hands against his ears.

He went to the small nightstand next to the bed and opened the drawer. Angel's eyes darted to the door, but the full weight of his body was on her before she could move off the bed. His hand gripped her arm and pushed it roughly against one of the posts of the bed. Thin white rope squeezed her skin. When he moved to the other arm, she bucked widely, trying to throw him off and free her hand. It was in vain. Her other hand was pushed against the other post and the rope yanked so hard against her wrists she yelled out in pain.

He got off the bed and took several deep breaths to calm himself. "You will be mine in every way, Angel. You won't get away. The sooner you realize it, the easier it will be. I wanted this to be a special time for us, but if you want to fight me, I will enjoy it just the same." A wild and dangerous glint flickered in his eyes as they glanced slowly from the top of her head to the tip of her bare toes.

The hope of freedom she'd desperately clung to the moment she woke up slipped away from her, like sand through her fingers. Despair squeezed around her, sucking the air from her lungs until it hurt to breathe. No one knew she was here. There was no escape.

CHAPTER 35

Bren chugged another cup of black coffee, its bitter taste stinging his tongue. Another six hours had passed and there was still no sign of Angel or her captor.

He looked over the case files until his eyes refused to see more.

One thing he knew for certain—it was someone who knew her, who knew about Meredith's case. *But who? And why?*

The bartender had had two encounters with him, but never saw his face clearly. Bren left Angel's office, in search of Johnson in the MIR. "Do you have the bartender's address?"

Johnson nodded. "Why?"

"I want to speak with him. See if I can trigger a memory of his run-in with the possible killer."

Johnson's stern gaze raked over him. "That was a dead end."

Bren shoved his hands in his pocket. "Look, I'm trying every possible lead."

Johnson sat still for several seconds before he stood up. "Alright then. Let's get on with it."

They headed to the parking lot, taking Johnson's patrol car.

"Why do you think Jeff's statement will be any different than the first time around?" Johnson asked.

Bren shrugged. "I don't, but I'm hoping he might

remember something about the killer the night he saw him at the bar. Certain memories can take longer to manifest themselves than others. We might get lucky."

Johnson didn't seem convinced. His eyes remained on the road ahead of him.

Bren wasn't sure how he'd proceed when they pulled into what he assumed was the parking lot of the bartender's apartment complex.

They got out of the car and Bren followed Johnson to the door with the number four.

"Constable Johnson?" Jeff glanced between Johnson and Bren. "What's going on?"

"We want to have a word with you about the night the first victim was murdered," Johnson answered.

Jeff stepped aside so they could enter. His face was still black and blue and he limped to the couch. "How can I help?"

"What do you recall about the man you saw with the first victim?" Bren asked.

Jeff ran a hand along his stubbly chin. "As I said in my statement, it was dark and I couldn't see his face."

"You mentioned he had long hair? Could you tell where he might have come from?"

Jeff looked between them with what Bren assumed was annoyance at having to repeat himself.

"As I told the other officer, I couldn't see anything."

Johnson went to stand before him. "We believe he has Angel."

Jeff shifted his weight on the couch. "Bloody hell!"

Bren couldn't agree more.

Jeff's face scrunched and he closed his eyes as if he were concentrating on something. "If I had to choose, I'd say Mediterranean or some Spanish country, but I'm not certain." The frustration in his voice was evident.

Jeff's answer wasn't what Bren had hoped for, but it was something.

"Thanks for your time," Johnson said. "Please call us if you recall anything else." He handed Jeff his card.

"I will," Jeff assured them.

They let themselves out and headed back to the police car.

"Well, that was a bit of a disaster," Johnson said once they were inside the car.

"I'm sorry for wasting your time."

"Don't worry yourself. We did get something, even if it wasn't what we'd hoped for."

Bren couldn't agree with him, but he appreciated the gesture. The other possibility on his list was the police database. Not everyone had access to the case information, so someone either hacked into the system to get the information or they had inside contacts to get that information. That meant it could be another officer, but what was their motive? He racked his brain for some other way the general public could get their hands on the information.

Daniel Rumson! He was conniving enough, but what was his motive?

"Is it possible that Daniel Rumson managed to get the details of Meredith's case?"

Johnson gave him a sideways glance. "It's possible, but it's highly doubtful he'd get them all."

"There's only one way to find out."

"If we speak with him, I ask all the questions. Got it?"

"I can't make any promises." Bren's eyes met his squarely.

Johnson shook his head. "Well, at least you're honest."

Instead of heading back to the police station, Johnson turned down a road that would take them to Daniel's workplace.

When they arrived at the Cayman Newsroom station, Daniel was on the air.

"In local news, the Meredith Mason copycat killer is still

on the loose. How many more people will have to die before the police arrest the person responsible? We all know who it is. Are the police protecting one of their own?"

Johnson tensed next to him. It was no secret that only a few people on the force, himself included, didn't suspect Angel of the crime.

Daniel finished his segment and smiled snidely when he saw them. He gestured them towards his office.

"Professor MacDougal, Constable Johnson. What brings you here?"

"We're here to ask you about Meredith's cases and how much you know," Bren said.

"Everything, of course," he replied arrogantly. "I make it my business to know all the details when I'm doing a story."

"Is it true you harassed Angel and her aunt when you first started at CNR?" Johnson asked.

"I didn't harass them," Daniel said defensively. "I merely asked them questions."

"We're going to need to see the questions you asked, along with any other information in your possession relating to Meredith's case and her family," Johnson said.

"Why? Are the police finally coming to the same realization I did?"

"What realization?" Bren asked, although he suspected.

"Like mother, like daughter?"

"No." Johnson's tight jawline clenched. "Inspector Angel has disappeared and we think the copycat killer has her."

Bren knew that under normal circumstances Johnson wouldn't have shared information about the case, but these weren't normal circumstances.

Daniel laughed. "Disappeared? How convenient."

Bren closed the distance between them and gripped Daniel's shirt collar. "Her aunt was killed and now she's gone. I'm going to do everything in my power to find her, even if that means pounding what you learned out of you. Got it?"

Daniel smiled. "I guess I was right about your relationship?"

Bren raised one of his fists, but Johnson interrupted. "We'd appreciate your cooperation, but I can get a search warrant if need be."

"That won't be necessary. I'm happy to assist the department however I can, with the condition that I get the exclusive of interviewing Ang—the killer—when captured."

"That's not something I can promise, but I'll see what I can do," Johnson said in his best English tone.

"Not good enough." Daniel crossed his arms. "It'll take you days, maybe even weeks to get a warrant."

God, he hated this guy. "I'll give you the exclusive on the case, from an insider perspective," Bren said. "But it better be good and not a waste of my time, otherwise I call it off."

"The files are at my apartment," Daniel said, seemingly satisfied with the answer he got.

"Let's go," Johnson said.

Daniel collected something from his desk before following Bren and Johnson outside. Daniel drove his own car and Bren and Johnson waited by Daniel's flat door until he arrived.

When he did, Bren and Johnson followed close behind him and waited in the living room while he got the files from this office.

"You sure that's everything?" Johnson asked.

"Yes."

"Are you sure you're not hiding anything?" Bren asked.

"Nothing. You'll see the truth when you review all the information for yourself."

Bren wanted to knock him on his ass just to get that smug look off his face. But he needed to stay focused to find Angel. The chances of her survival decreased the more time that passed.

He took the chair next to Johnson at the dining table.

"Did you find any records of mental illness in her family?" He and Johnson hadn't found much, but few records were kept on mental patients.

"The only mental one in the family was Meredith. I spoke with the rest of the family and no one remembers anyone else having mental issues."

They could've lied to him, but it was strange they couldn't find anything. According to Maisy, more than one woman in their family had had a mental breakdown. Surely someone would've remembered?

"Did you know that Maisy had a child very few people know about?" Daniel said offhandedly.

"Come again?" Johnson asked.

"The birth certificate didn't give me much detail, but I spoke with Maisy's cousin, who was happy to tell me all the details since they don't get along," Daniel said with a smirk.

"Was it a boy or a girl?"

"It was a boy. Apparently she kept the relationship a secret because the father was married. That's why she gave the baby away. Maisy didn't want anyone knowing she had a child with a married man."

"What was the man's name?" Bren asked.

Daniel smiled in a way that said he was in control. "Lorenzo Sanchez Hernandez."

Bren and Johnson looked at each other.

"Quite a coincidence, isn't it?" Daniel said with a smirk.

Neither said a word, waiting to see what more Daniel had to say before jumping to conclusions.

"I checked it out and turns out that Constable Sanchez's father's name was Lorenzo Sanchez Hernandez, and he worked in Cayman for two years before returning to his family in Honduras. Now, either his wife had an affair while he was working here, or he took Maisy's child back with him."

Bren's mind raced with questions about Sanchez. *Did he*

know he was related to Angel? He never hid the fact he was attracted to Angel, but this? Why wouldn't Daniel make that information public? Surely it would've created scandal for Angel and her aunt, not to mention Sanchez.

From the perplexed expression on Johnson's face, Bren could tell he was thinking the same thing. He stood up and gestured for Bren to do the same. He picked up the file from the table. "Thank you for your time, Mr. Rumson."

"What? You're leaving?" Daniel asked, as if expecting them to share more police information with him.

"We'll contact you if we have any more questions." Johnson headed towards the door.

One question was burning a hole in Bren's brain. "Why didn't you go public with the Sanchez information?"

Daniel's cocky expression disappeared. "I didn't want to tarnish his reputation."

Bren knew from the look in his eyes it was more than that. He was scared of Sanchez. Daniel didn't strike him as the type to back down easily, so either Sanchez had something serious on him, or he had threatened Daniel to keep quiet.

He and Johnson headed towards the door, ignoring the questions Daniel shouted at them as they left.

"Are you thinking what I'm thinking?" Bren asked when they reached the parking lot.

"I've known Sanchez for two years. I can't believe he'd do something like this."

"But..." Bren was certain there was a "but" in there somewhere.

"I always thought his obsession with Angel was...odd," he said tentatively.

"He did have access to the case information," Bren pointed out.

"I'm not saying another word until we speak with CS Williams."

Bren nodded in agreement and got in his car. His mind

went over every conversation he had with Sanchez, looking for clues to his behavior. If Sanchez was Maisy's son, that meant he and Angel were related. *Why would he pursue her unless it was to detract from the truth they were related?*

He'd been at Maisy's murder scene. If she was his mother, he didn't show any signs of sadness or an inkling of emotion that might indicate he was close to her. If he'd taken Angel, why would he have shown up to work today? Nothing made sense.

There was only one person who had the answers to all the questions he, and now Johnson, had. Sanchez.

The silence in the car ride back to the police station was brutal, but neither of them broke it, lost in their own sea of questions about Sanchez and his connection to Angel and possibly the case.

Bren followed closely behind Johnson as he headed straight to Williams' office. They walked in, not bothering to knock. Ebanks was sitting in one of the chairs before his desk.

"What did you find?" Williams asked.

"Where's Sanchez?" Johnson asked.

"He left. I believe his vacation started today. Why?"

Johnson and Bren recounted what they learned from Daniel and how they came to the conclusion he might be the copycat killer.

"Sanchez? But why?" Williams stood up and went towards the door.

"This killer is obsessed with Meredith's cases and life, so it's not a stretch that obsession would include Angel. Maybe her rejection pushed him over the edge. We won't know the truth until we find Angel." Bren yanked open the office door and headed out, Williams close on his heels.

"Ebanks, you're coming with us," Williams barked as they treaded past the clutter of desks and constables.

A flurry of conversation erupted behind them as they exited the room, passed the reception area, and headed out.

Bren got in the front seat of Williams' car.

"Meet me at Sanchez's house," Williams ordered Ebanks.

Ebanks eyed him and then Williams.

"You got a hearing problem?" he barked.

"No sir," he replied quickly, getting into the car next to them.

Dread crushed Bren's chest as he buckled his seat belt. As they sped to save Angel, he prayed they'd get to her in time.

CHAPTER 36

Sanchez wanted to punch a hole in the bathroom wall. Things weren't going according to his plan. He hated when things didn't go according to plan. She didn't understand everything he'd done for her, had said so with her disgust-filled eyes. *Didn't she know what he'd sacrificed for her?* He cleaned the gash in his leg, put ointment on it, and wrapped it with a bandage.

He shouldn't have put the corkscrew within her reach. He'd thought he could trust her when he saw her wearing one of the dresses he'd picked out for her and was sitting on the couch instead of by the door, ready to ambush him. When he'd seen she was waiting for him, his heart had soared and all he could think of was getting close to her, holding her in his arms, and then beneath him in the bedroom he'd prepared for her.

The moment she elbowed him and stabbed him, he knew he was wrong. Rage had filled him and he'd wanted to strangle her and cut her throat the way she had sliced his heart. He'd wanted to rip her clothes from her body and hurt her when she thrashed wildly against him to get free.

He'd imagined their first time much differently. Soft music, candlelight, and her smiling down at him as they made love. But she'd ruined that and now she had to pay.

A knock on the front door interrupted his thoughts. His heartbeat stuttered as he limped to answer it. He pulled his pants leg down, checked to make sure no blood was on it. He calmed his features and opened the door.

"Sir? Professor? What's going on? Did you find Angel?" he asked eagerly.

"Where the hell is she?" Bren demanded, trying to push past Williams to get inside Sanchez's apartment.

"Back off, Bren, or you'll be waiting in the car," Williams warned.

Bren mumbled incoherently.

"How the hell should I know where Angel is?"

Williams pushed himself inside the house, not waiting to be invited in. "We have reason to believe you're responsible for her disappearance."

"What makes you say that?"

"You picked an interesting time to start your vacation, and—"

Sanchez laughed. "Is this a joke?"

Bren stepped closer to where they stood. "You didn't let him finish. He was going to add that you're obsessed with Angel."

"Obsessed? Is he for real, sir?" Sanchez looked at Williams.

"Why didn't you tell anyone you're Maisy's son?" Williams asked.

Damned nosy reporter. He'd hope to keep that part of his life secret. He shrugged. "Yeah, so?"

"Don't you find that strange? Being related to Angel and not telling her. Wanting to date her?" Bren's penetrating gaze bore into him, studying Sanchez like he was a patient.

"I wasn't trying to date her, just ease her into the truth." It was an easy lie, but he could tell it didn't convince Bren.

"Are you sure you didn't kill her when she found out the truth?" Bren pressed.

"Kill her? I loved her like a sister!" Sanchez defended.

"What about Maisy? Did you love her too?" Williams asked.

"I didn't know Maisy," he said as casually as he could muster, even as anger boiled below the surface.

"Did you confront Maisy about giving you up?" Bren asked.

"I spoke with her about it because I wanted to meet the woman who gave birth to me." He shrugged as if it didn't matter.

"That's right. And now she's dead," Williams inserted.

Sanchez clenched his jaw. *He should've killed that reporter when he had the chance.* "I didn't kill Maisy."

"You going somewhere?" Williams asked, taking in his formal attire.

Sanchez shrugged. "Thinking about it."

Williams walked around the apartment, his head cocked as if listening for noises.

Sanchez chuckled to himself. *This house is solid concrete. You're not going to hear anything.*

"Where were you last night?" Williams asked.

"Here."

"Were you alone?" he glared at Sanchez.

"No. I had three women with me who can vouch for my ironclad alibi." Sanchez smirked. He stepped towards the couch slowly, making sure to show no sign of the pain from the wound in his leg. "Sir, you've known me for five years, before I came to Cayman. Why would I do this? You know how ambitious I am. Would I seriously risk it all by kidnapping my superior officer?"

Williams' face scrunched in thought and, Sanchez suspected, doubt. Sanchez wanted to smile.

"You'd take that risk if you were obsessed with her," Bren cut in.

Sanchez's fingernails gripped the edge of the couch as he shifted his weight. *Damn, he hated that man!*

"Why would I want Angel? I'm never in need of a date any day of the week."

"She doesn't want you. That's reason enough for a man like you."

Sanchez gritted his teeth. "A man like me?" He envisioned stabbing Bren with the same corkscrew Angel had stabbed him with.

"One who can't accept defeat or the fact that a woman isn't interested in anything you're offering."

Sanchez shrugged casually, but in his mind he'd put a bullet through Bren's brain and watched him die in a bloody puddle at his feet. "Think what you want. I've got no trouble getting women."

Bren looked at Williams before taking a tentative step towards Sanchez. "This isn't about other women. This is about you being obsessed with Angel, doing anything to get her, including murdering those women." His brogue thickened with the anger in his tone.

Sanchez laughed despite pangs of fear. "Is he serious?" He glanced towards Williams and then back to Bren. "An officer protects people, not kills them, Professor," he said, using the words Angel had said to him. "Another problem with your theory is that I don't have Angel."

"Oh, she's here," Bren insisted.

Sanchez waved his arm in a circle. "Feel free to search my house if you like," he taunted.

Bren gritted his teeth and took a menacing step towards him, as if to attack him, but stopped and squeezed his fists at his side instead.

Sanchez wanted to laugh. Bren wasn't worthy of Angel. If someone had taken Angel from him, he'd have hauled him by his neck and thrown him out the nearest window. He leaned back in the printed cushions as Bren, Williams, Johnson, and Ebanks checked his house for Angel. He even heard Bren call out her name a couple of times, as if she'd answer him because she was behind the wall. *Did Bren think he was stupid?*

***

Bren closed the closet door of Sanchez's third bedroom. *Nothing!* They hadn't found a damn thing. Not a single sign or hint that Angel was even dragged through the house. He should have known better. Sanchez had been pedantic about the crime scenes; he wouldn't drop his guard now, even after getting what he wanted.

He went through every room and then out into the backyard, looking for any signs of an underground storage area or something in the house, but there was nothing. More than anything, he wanted to grab Sanchez by the neck and beat the truth out of him, but that wasn't an option.

If only he knew more about Sanchez, he would know how to handle him long enough for Angel to make it out alive.

His stomach lurched and fear gripped him when he remembered the stories of women who'd been kept captive for more than a month. Pain pierced his chest and his tongue was a sour rag in his mouth at the thought of Angel going through what those women had.

He leaned against the outside of the house and took deep breaths.

"You alright?" Williams stood before him, his eyes filled with concern.

"Aye, fine." Bren stood upright. "Did you find something?" he asked, despite already knowing the answer.

"Nothing." Williams ran a hand over his chin. It was then Bren noticed the shadow of unshaven hair and his bloodshot eyes. He'd been so concerned with his own pain he hadn't stopped to consider how Angel's disappearance had effected Williams.

"We can't arrest him on suspicion only," Williams said, and headed back inside.

Bren followed him through the backdoor. "I know."

Inside the house, Johnson and Ebanks stood by the front

door, awaiting orders. Ebanks was chatting casually with Sanchez, as if they were paying a social call instead of investigating him.

"Find anything?" Sanchez asked snidely.

Bren didn't answer, afraid he would punch him.

Sanchez laughed. "One minute it's kidnapping and now murder? You've got one sick imagination, Professor." He leaned against the couch. "I had no motive for killing those women."

"That part I can't figure out. Maybe it has something to do with Maisy?"

The lines in his brow twitched. "What about her?"

"She's your mother. That makes Angel your cousin. That's sick!" Bren said with conviction.

"You don't know what you're talking about."

"How did it feel to kill your own mother, Sanchez?" Bren taunted.

"She might've given birth to me, but she was never my mother," he said quietly.

"Is that why you killed her and those women? You killed those women to gain the courage to kill your mother?"

Sanchez remained silent.

"Anything to report?" Williams asked when Johnson returned.

Bren shook his head.

"I guess you were wrong, Professor," Sanchez taunted from the couch.

Arrogant bastard! He'd done nothing but sit on the couch the whole time they were there. It was the first thing he did when they... Something clicked in Bren's brain. He was sitting. He rarely sat. He liked exerting the fact he was taller than most people by looking down at them, intimidating them. *Why was he sitting now instead of in his face taunting him with his victory?*

"You feeling alright, Sanchez?"

Narrowed eyebrows scrutinized him. "I'm fine."

"Really?" Bren moved to where he sat on the couch and looked down at him. "Any reason why you chose to sit the whole time we've been here?"

They all shot Bren a strange look.

"Is it a crime to sit now?" Sanchez joked.

"No, but it's a good way to hide the fact you can't stand properly."

Williams looked at Sanchez and then back at him, a smile forming. "Sanchez, would you please stand and walk across the room."

Sanchez laughed. "You can't be serious."

"I'm very serious."

"This is ridiculous!" Sanchez insisted.

"It's a trivial thing and won't take a minute of your time."

Sanchez shifted his position on the couch and, to Bren's dismay, got up with no sign of pain on his face, even when he walked across the room.

"Happy now?"

Williams seemed unconvinced. "Again," he stated.

Sanchez looked at Dustin with wide eyes. Pleading eyes, or so it seemed to Bren.

Bren's heart raced as he waited for Sanchez to walk across the room again and give them a sign. Angel had left her mark on him. It wasn't showing up anywhere visible and they couldn't ask him to strip so this was their only option.

Sanchez's tan face grew paler with every step he took and beads of sweat started to break out above his top lip and on his forehead. The relief on his face was obvious when he reached the other side of the room.

"Again," Williams insisted.

"The hell I will!" Sanchez shouted. His face was flushed and sweaty.

"How about I have Ebanks and Johnson drag you

downtown and book you in for questioning for the murder of Angel's aunt?" Williams threatened, his tone deadly calm.

"Based on what evidence?"

"We might not be able to hold you, but the damage of being questioned for murder won't be soon forgotten, especially when being considered for a promotion."

Sanchez made a fist at his side. "You bastard!"

"Insulting an officer?" Williams dared him to say more.

"I'll sue you and the police department!"

"I'm weeks away from retirement. I'll be gone before your case reaches court."

It was then Bren saw the drop of blood on the white tile next to Sanchez's brightly polished black shoes.

"We've got you!" Bren said in triumph, even as Sanchez's eyes grew dark and his face contorted with malice. He was still looking down at the floor when he heard Williams shout his name and felt the impact of Sanchez's tall frame crash into his. The sound of bones crushing echoed in the room as they both hit the tiled floor.

CHAPTER 37

Sanchez's fists hit the back of his head several times before he could roll over to throw back a few of his own.

Williams and the constables stepped forward to break them up. "Back off!" he shouted and hoped they would give him a couple of minutes with Sanchez before pulling them apart. He rammed his fist into Sanchez's face several times before he countered and then took a few from him. They scrambled off the floor and attacked each other again with their feet, arms, elbows—anything that was free and visible.

"Where is she?" Bren shouted when he finally got Sanchez in a headlock.

"Go to hell!"

"That's where you'll be heading if ye don't tell me where she is." Bren indicated that he intended to make good on his threat by tightening his grip around Sanchez's neck, squeezing it harder until he knew he couldn't breathe and would soon pass out. He loosened his grip and Sanchez gasped for air.

"I was wrestling champion at high school and college so I can do this all day, Sanchez."

"Fuc—"

Bren changed his grip on Sanchez quickly so he had him in an arm bar. "You don't answer me and I'll break your arm—painfully," Bren threatened.

"Bren," Williams warned. Bren knew he was going too far, but he wasn't about to stop now. Angel could be hurt and bleeding, or worse, trapped in a space with no air where she would die if they didn't get to her in time.

"Tell me, you bastard!"

Sanchez screamed in pain, but still didn't budge. Bren squeezed tighter.

"Bren, stop!" Williams warned a second time. Johnson and Ebanks would be pulling them apart soon and he wouldn't let them until he got his answer.

Bren squeezed tighter. The sound of crunching filled the room and Sanchez screamed. "She's behind the wall in my bedroom," he whispered in defeat.

Bren loosened his grip quickly and pushed Sanchez away from him, disgusted. "He's all yours," he said.

Bren stood up, and headed to the back of the house to Sanchez's bedroom. He looked closer at the walls for a seam, a crack. Something—anything. He didn't see a thing. He looked around the room and noticed a large armoire. Sanchez had a walk-in closet and a wall-mounted TV; Bren wondered what he would need with an armoire. He strode over to it and yanked on the handles, but they didn't open. His heart raced as he pushed against it, but it didn't budge. Angel was just behind this wall and he couldn't get to her.

"Do you need help?" Johnson asked from the doorway.

"What do you think?"

Bren's shoulders slumped and he took a deep breath. "How about giving me a hand with this thing?"

"I thought you'd never ask."

Johnson moved to stand next to him and together they pushed against the armoire. Again it didn't budge.

"There must be a lever or something that moves it," Bren suggested.

Johnson nodded in agreement and ran his hand along the edge. There was a click and then it moved, revealing a dark space. Bren reached in and found a light switch.

"Stay here," Bren said.

"That's not going to happen," Johnson insisted.

"Look, this isn't about me. It's about Angel and leaving her with a little dignity."

Johnson took his meaning and agreed. "Shout if you need me."

Bren nodded. He prayed Angel was down there and that Sanchez hadn't led them to a dead end. What he prayed for most was that she was unharmed and alive.

***

Angel stretched, testing the rope, hoping to find a weakness in the knots she had been tied in or the bedposts the ropes were tied to. Nothing. She yanked harder, wincing when the rope cut deeper into her skin. It was no use.

She threw her head against the pillow in frustration. Sanchez surprised her by leaving her alone. It must have been to bandage the wound she'd given him with the corkscrew. It would buy her time, but would it be enough time for her to be found?

She ground her teeth. She should've been smarter and seen Sanchez for what he was. The warning signs were there: His forceful grips, pushiness to the point of crassness, and his leery gaze when she caught him staring at her. Why hadn't she taken the signs of his obsession more seriously?

She'd let the problems in her own life with the curse, and Bren's reappearance in her life, cloud her judgment and life instead of focusing her attention on the case. *Stupid!*

She banged her head against the pillow again. "Stop feeling sorry for yourself and find a way to get yourself the hell out of here!" she yelled at herself.

The click of a door opening in the distance set Angel's heart racing. *He was back.* She pulled at the ropes again, but the only result was her skin burning.

Dread filled her stomach, heavy and sour. *This was it.*

Sanchez was coming to claim his prize. Defeat crushed her hard and furious until she couldn't breathe.

The footsteps came closer and grew louder. Then a voice called out.

"Angel?"

It was Bren! She sank back into the pillow and a feeling of weightlessness washed over her. The urge to laugh and cry at once erupted within her. "I'm here," she said, but the words were just above a whisper.

"Angel!" Bren rushed to the side of the bed and pulled at the ropes. She winced in pain.

"Sorry."

"Don't worry about it—just get them off me!" she pleaded.

She watched him go to work on the ropes, his face hard and determined. He never looked better. Her heart swelled with all the love she felt. He'd found her.

She wrapped her arms around him when they were loose and she didn't let go. She didn't protest when he picked her up off the bed and carried her in his arms up the stairs to her freedom.

***

"Angel, wait! You can't leave me! We belong together," Sanchez pleaded when he saw her in Bren's arms.

Bren set Angel down and she strode up to Sanchez, who was being constrained by Ebanks. She slapped his sharply across the face. "I don't belong anywhere near you, you sick bastard!"

She then leaned in and whispered something in his ear. His eyes widened in surprise, and shifted to hurt and then pure hatred. His gaze moved between Bren and then back at Angel.

Sanchez caught them all off guard when he broke free and reached for Angel. Ebanks pushed her out of the way and reached for Sanchez, but caught only air. Sanchez then flung himself at Johnson, throwing him against the wall. His head cracked against the concrete and he slumped to the floor.

Bren now lunged at Sanchez and their bodies crashed into each other hard and fast, landing on the floor. Bren yelled in pain when something was rammed into his side. He couldn't see it, but from the pain, he knew it wasn't Sanchez's fist. He felt it again and again before it stopped. When he looked up, Sanchez stood over him, hatred burning in his eyes as Williams finally constrained him.

"You don't deserve her! She should be mine!" Sanchez bellowed, pushing against the arms that held him.

Bren couldn't answer. He was lightheaded from the loss of blood. He looked down at his side and saw a corkscrew protruding from his shirt, which was stained red and spreading. He leaned back against the tile floor and heard Williams say, "Call 911" and Angel screaming his name. He saw her blurred figure hovering over him before he blacked out.

CHAPTER 38

Angel set down the manila envelope and took a seat in the chair in front of Williams' desk. The DNA results from Jackson. He'd offered to tell her, but she had wanted to wait and find out with Williams. Part of her was excited Williams might be her father; another was anxious. Just wrapping her head around it gave her a headache.

"Is that what I think it is?" he asked, nodding towards the envelope.

"Yes."

"Are you sure you want to know?" His expression reflected her trepidation.

He was nervous too. She felt better. She'd gotten past the dislike she felt towards him in her childhood, but it would still be a big adjustment for both of them. She knew in her heart it was an adjustment she was willing to make. Was he?

Angel nodded. Her breath hitched in her throat as he opened the envelope. His expression remained unreadable as he scanned the document and she longed to jump up and down like a kid in a candy store about to get more candy than they were usually allowed.

It had been three days since she was saved from Sanchez and also the curse. She'd had the best sleep of her life in the nights since, waking each day with a sense of happiness and hope she'd never felt before. Despite what Sanchez did, he did break the curse.

"Looks like I'm retiring early," Williams said, and leaned back in his chair.

"Why?" *What did his retiring early have to do with the DNA tests?*

"A daughter reporting to her father on a police force might not go over so well, even on an island as small as this one." A smile lit up his face, despite his efforts to contain it. "Are you surprised?"

His smile had taken her by surprise. The skin around his eyes crinkled, but he looked younger, showing signs of what Maisy and Meredith must have once seen in him. She didn't know what to say.

His eyes held hers, as if asking if she was happy or disappointed. Their relationship had changed considerably in the past few weeks.

Her hands fidgeted in her lap. "No. I suspected."

"Will you miss me?"

"Your position may be easy to replace, but you're not."

She reached across the table to touch his hand. He was the only family she had left who hadn't shunned her. She still had questions.

"What happened between you and my mother?" The voices had stopped for her. Had they stopped for Meredith?

He moved his hand away and pain filled his eyes.

"She tried to tell me what was happening to her, but I didn't believe her. I thought she was going crazy, so I pushed her away, until she left me. It's when you get to the end of your life that you realize the mistakes that you made and feel the regrets of the risks you didn't take." He looked at Angel. "I should have fought for you. I should have known that your mother didn't have another man in her life."

The sting of tears came but for once she didn't push them back, but let them fall freely. Meredith couldn't be saved from the place in life the curse had taken her. She had lost Meredith, her mother, but she had just gained a father.

"You were both in a lot of pain," Angel defended.

"That's a pitiful excuse and you know it!"

"True, but you have time to make it up to me and that's all that matters."

He smiled and offered his hand. She took it. It was time for a new start.

After setting a day and time for their first father-daughter date, Angel stood up to leave.

"Don't live your life with regret, Angel. You have your life back. Don't let it go to waste."

She gave him a weak smile. *Bren.* Would he give them a chance after everything she had put him through?

CHAPTER 39

The gentle touch of a hand woke him. Bren opened his eyes to find Angel sitting by his bed.

"How you feeling?" she asked, brushing a stray hair from his face.

"Better."

This was the first time since he'd arrived at the hospital that they'd been alone. His room was usually filled with police constables coming to pay their respects or ask him questions, as well as nurses and doctors checking up on him.

"What happened to Sanchez?" he asked.

Angel smiled. "He's at Northward for now, but Williams is working to get him sent to England."

Bren wanted to laugh, but knew it would hurt if he did. "Did he ever confess to murdering those women?"

She shook her head. "But we found copies of Meredith's case files in the house where he held me. Between the kidnapping charges, my statement, and what we found at his house, everyone's certain it's enough to convict him."

He eased his head back into the pillow. Sanchez was gone and wouldn't be able to get to Angel. That was all that mattered.

She placed her hand in his. When their eyes met, he was surprised to see her unguarded emotions shining in her eyes. His heart raced with hope.

"It's gone," she blurted.

"What's gone?"

"The voices. The curse." She smiled radiantly, her entire face lighting up.

The psychiatrist in him was thinking it was impossible, but the man who loved Angel remained silent, waiting for her explanation with a small sliver of hope she might be right.

"Maisy was behind the curse."

It didn't make any sense even as she explained it to him, especially the part of how the voices stopped after Sanchez put a bullet through Maisy's brain. "I forgave my mother," she continued. She told him her suspicions that her mother might be cured now too, but knew that it was too late for her mother, for their relationship. Tears filled her eyes.

She shifted on the bed to get more comfortable. "I haven't had a drink, or the urge to drink," she said, and touched his face lovingly. "My dreams have been peaceful— sweet—with images of you and me."

He couldn't find a response. The joy that he and Angel had a glimpse of a future together burst inside him, making him speechless.

"I'll go to AA meetings, or see a psychiatrist if you need me to, Bren. Whatever it takes to make you believe I'm telling the truth, to make you believe that I'll do anything to have a life with you."

She lifted his hand and pressed it against her face. Before she could say another word, he blurted, "I love you."

The doubt that had clouded her eyes disappeared and was replaced with happiness. "I loved you the moment you made me laugh." She kissed his hand softly. "I'm sorry I tried to leave you. I promise not to leave you again."

"I understand why you did it," Bren said softly.

"Really? Why?"

"The only other person you loved was a killer who betrayed you. You didn't know if you'd be one or that you might kill the man you love. Does that about sum it up?" He gave her a crooked grin.

She touched his nose playfully. "Still trying to analyze me, Bren?"

He pressed the button so the bed adjusted, bringing her closer to him. "Always, forever," he whispered before he kissed her.

ABOUT THE AUTHOR

Subscribe to Elke's quarterly newsletter to find out about her latest releases, special deals, appearances, and contests.

Contract Elke
Email: hotcaymanmama@yahoo.com
Website: http://elkefeuer.com
Twitter: @ElkeFeuer
Facebook: https://www.facebook.com/pages/Elke-Feuer/185367964831994

Keep reading for a special look at the debut novel of Elke Feuer from Crimson Romance.

COMING SOON

For The Love of Jazz

Prologue

CHICAGO 1959

Please meet me, it's important! *Lola pulls her knee-length coat closer to her petite frame and suppresses the tickle of fear at the base of her spine. It's late, but she can't ignore her friend's urgent request.*

Cool night air rustling through the trees is the only noise. Visitors to the park are gone, leaving behind dark empty walkways and overflowing garbage bins. Crunching leaves and strange noises in the black distance start her heart racing. This is a bad idea.

She sees her friend coming and smiles in welcome and relief. As they draw closer, there is no smile in return. Normally cool but inviting eyes shine with malice. Lola's eyes widen in surprise as a gun is pointed at her. Before she can scream she feels the sting and burning of flesh as bullets from the outstretched gun enter her shoulder once, twice. She falls to her knees.

Her eyes fill with horror as reality sets in. "Why?"

Silent hate glares from behind the barrel of the gun and another bullet fires, this time hitting her leg.

227

"Help!" she screams. Her gaze shifts frantically down lonely sidewalks. No one is coming. It crushes her like the pain tearing her apart.

Another shot fires and hits her other leg, and Lola knows she is meant to suffer first. She raises her hand in a frail attempt to stop the bullets. It doesn't make a difference. The gun fires again and blood pools around her and on the icy ground beneath her fingertips.

Hot tears spill as she thinks of William. If she'd listened to her intuition, she could be spooned against him instead of dying in the dirt like an animal abandoned by its owner.

She doesn't want to die and leave him, or the happiness she's found. She screams until her lungs burn with the sensation they'll burst from the strain.

Anger boils the blood still running through her veins. She longs to take the gun and shoot back. Have them feel her pain. Feel the agony of regret; words left unspoken, unshared kisses, things left undone, the fear of the unknown that lies in the darkness swirling in the distance, and the anguish of the unanswered question. 'Why?'

She remembers the offered friendship, smiles, and the laughter shared. It was all a lie! Heartache crushes her, dulling the pain of her physical wounds. "This isn't over," she vows, even as life begins to drain from her weak frame.

"You're over," is spat back at her.

Images of the moment she met William, their first kiss, and their lovemaking flicker like a movie before her closed eyes. She won't share the rest of this life with him, bear his children, or grow old with him, but she takes comfort in knowing she'll see him again, love him again, and no one will take it away. She clings to the hope she can wait for William until they are together again. Yes, she will wait. Silent calm seeps in as her life slips away.

CHAPTER 1

"This is it." Josie Fagan took a deep breath. "Moment of truth."

She got out of her car, ran shaky fingers through her hair, and smiled when it tickled the back of her neck. The curls would return to their original state, but the gesture gave her comfort.

Each step to the chestnut brick house made her heartbeat escalate. She'd felt a connection the moment she saw it advertised for renovations - even dreamed about the house and a man standing in the upstairs window, waving her inside. She looked up, but no one was there.

Emotional connections, as her father used to call them, were as natural to her as breathing. Since her childhood, she'd felt strong connections to things like jazz music, old buildings, and, just recently, Chicago. Like being black, it was a part of who she was.

She made her way along the sidewalk to the crimson front door and, with a shaky hand, rang the doorbell.

When it opened, she looked up to meet cool emerald eyes and neatly combed ebony hair. If not for his suit, she'd have guessed he was a construction worker, with his strong square jawline, and shoulders that were barely contained beneath his expensive suit. Icicles of recognition jumped across her vertebrae.

She extended her hand. "Patrick Pullman?"

When he took her hand, memories sparkled in his daunting stare before he released her hand reluctantly, as though breaking the grasp would stop the wheels turning in his mind. "Yes. Josie Fagan?"

Interesting. He felt it, too. She nodded, but pretended not to notice. Her interest was in what lay behind him. She was about to see the inside of the house that had taunted her the last two days. The intensity of the connection to it surprised her. Other than jazz music, no connection had been stronger.

He gestured her inside.

When she stepped into the entryway, warmth surrounded her like the coverlet her mother had given her on her eighteenth birthday. It started in the pit of her stomach and spread prickles over the surface of her skin. It was the thrill of waiting for the sun to set, then watching it explode into brilliant hues of red, yellow, and gold. It was being curled up with her favorite book by the warm glow of a fireplace with the faint sounds of jazz in the background. It was home.

Click here to buy